BRIDGE OF FEAR

BRIDGE OF FEAR

Dorothy Eden

Chivers Press   •   G.K. Hall & Co.
Bath, England   Waterville, Maine USA

This Large Print edition is published by Chivers Press, England, and by G.K. Hall & Co., USA.

Published in 2001 in the U.K. by arrangement with the Author c/o David Higham.

Published in 2001 in the U.S. by arrangement with David Higham Associates, Inc.

U.K. Hardcover   ISBN 0-7540-4568-4   (Chivers Large Print)
U.K. Softcover   ISBN 0-7540-4569-2   (Camden Large Print)
U.S. Softcover   ISBN 0-7838-9500-3   (Nightingale Series Edition)

The text of this Large Print edition is unabridged.
Other aspects of the book may vary from the original edition.

Set in 16 pt. New Times Roman.

Printed in Great Britain on acid-free paper.

British Library Cataloguing in Publication Data available

Library of Congress Cataloging-in-Publication Data

Eden, Dorothy, 1912–
    Bridge of fear / by Dorothy Eden.
        p.   cm.
    ISBN 0-7838-9500-3 (lg. print : sc : alk. paper)
    1. British—Australia—Fiction. 2. Australia—Fiction.
    3. Large type books. I. Title.
    PR9639.3.E38 B75 2001
    823'.914—dc21   2001024483

For

Win and Bernie

Whose garden and kookaburras

I borrowed

BRIDGE OF FEAR

CHAPTER ONE

Again it was the harsh devilish laughter that woke Abby. She started up, shocked and tense. Then, opening her eyes fully, she slumped back dejectedly on the pillows.

It was the kookaburras in the jacaranda tree outside her window who were making the noise. There were three of them and they came every day to be fed. At first she had thought they were cute, with their plump bodies, beige and blue feathers, and black unwinking eyes fixed on the windows, waiting for a movement inside. It had amused her to lure them closer and closer with scraps of raw meat, taming their fierce shyness and wondering whether one day she would succeed in persuading them to eat out of her hand.

Luke said it couldn't be done, and that had made her more determined. It was as if, by taming the kookaburras, she would simultaneously overcome her own prejudice and hostility towards this new country.

But now she had had to admit her mistake. For the odd little trio, far from giving her any affection, took all they could get and when she was not there to feed them raised their hideous cacophony of sound, shattering her sleep morning after morning. It was strange that such cosy-looking birds were given that

1

strident laughter that seemed to deliberately mock everything soft and tender and decent, even love, perhaps particularly love. It was the voice of disillusion coming out of this primeval land.

Fully awake, Abby realized that Luke had gone. There was a faint depression in the pillow where his head had been, that was all. She leaned over, pressing her cheek against it. In the very first days of their marriage, when Luke had had to make an early start, she had insisted on getting up and getting his breakfast. But when he had gone she had had a never-ending day to face. His suggestion that he could make his own coffee and toast on these days, without disturbing her, had seemed practical after all. It wasn't as if he longed to have her waiting on him. Or as if he longed to have her at all . . .

That niggling doubt Abby pushed firmly away. But she had agreed that there was little point in her getting up early on these occasions. She could sleep until the kookaburras or some other strident noise woke her, and then at least a little more of the day would be gone.

For it seemed as if the hot bright days were simply an interval to be passed somehow until Luke's return at night. She tried not to let him see this, and indeed not to see it herself. She had a new attractive home, situated picturesquely on the banks of a tidal river. One

2

had to be near the water in Sydney, people told her, otherwise the summer heat was too oppressive. There was a natural swimming pool fenced off from any shark that might slide inconspicuously in from the wide blue waters of the harbor, and the garden, only half-developed, was there waiting for her to plan if she wished.

With housework, shopping, gardening, and idling in the hot sun she could very pleasantly fill in the days. Soon she would make friends. There were, after all, other people in Sydney besides the Moffatts who lived in the big stone house which stood up the hillside, towering over this modest new one like a mother over a child.

That was it, a watchful mother who wasn't sure what her new very modern and not particularly welcome child would get up to.

Old Mrs. Moffatt hadn't much wanted to sell this piece of land, Luke had told Abby. But circumstances had forced her to, so they must understand and try to be pleasant neighbors. It wasn't much fun having strangers come to live in your front garden.

But Lola, her daughter, didn't mind the strangers, Abby had noticed. Mary was more withdrawn and anyway had an invalid husband. But Lola . . .

Abby got out of bed abruptly, determined not to lie thinking. It was only nine o'clock. At the earliest, Luke would be home at seven that evening.

She would have a leisurely bath, then sit a long time over her coffee. After that she would tidy the house and go out shopping. Lunch was too easy, a salad and a fresh roll. She could plan a dinner that took a lot of preparation, so that a good part of the afternoon would be taken care of. Or she could swim, or go to the library, or take a ferry across the harbor into the city, sliding beneath the gigantic shadow of the bridge. Perhaps call at Luke's office and come home with him.

Only then Miss Atkinson, Luke's secretary, would look at her with her subtle reproach, thinking but not saying, 'Why aren't you at home cooking a meal for your husband? All this gadding about . . .'

One of the kookaburras outside the window, seeing movement within, gave an abrupt impatient cry.

'Be quiet!' Abby muttered. 'And stop staring. Why does everybody stare in this place?'

She didn't look up the hillside towards the stone house. Its windows might appear to be blank, but they wouldn't be. Either Mrs. Moffatt or the invalid son-in-law Milton would be looking out. Or Mary, but she would stand well back out of sight. She was more timid in her curiosity than the others. Lola would be at work. If Luke hadn't left too early he would have given her a lift, saving her from the

4

tedious journey by ferry.

It was a very natural thing to do. And he didn't always bring her home at night because, although she had a husband in San Francisco, or some place, she frequently spent the evening in town. She was a very attractive young woman . . . It was funny that Luke had never written to Abby about the Moffatts, when he seemed to be such a close friend of theirs. He had simply said:

'I've bought a piece of land down by the river. It's in one of Sydney's older suburbs, once very exclusive, but now slightly decayed. It's coming back, though, and this is a good investment.'

And later, 'The house is finished, we had a rush to get it ready before you arrived, but we've made it. Now that you're on the way I can't wait . . .'

But he hadn't said that Lola had helped him with the essential furnishings, carpets, chairs and tables, beds. The final touches were left for Abby who would want to choose her own colors. But the house had had to be liveable, and since Abby was arriving sooner than he had wanted her to, in spite of that impulsive, 'I can't wait . . .' someone had had to choose things. Lola had hoped she liked the all over carpet of dull green. It wouldn't clash with most colors, she had said. Like a garden with its permanent green background. But Australian gardens didn't have green

5

backgrounds. They were a flaunting riot of red and purple and amber, unless they were stony or red clay deserts where only the lizards thrived.

So Abby had come into the house that Luke had rushed to build and Lola to furnish. Because of all this expenditure she and Luke hadn't had a honeymoon, but had come straight here on their wedding night. And the Moffatts, all of them, including Deirdre, had been waiting with champagne. And no one had told Abby about the noise the kookaburras made early in the morning ...

That was eight weeks ago. She was settled now, Abby told herself. She had made cushions and hung curtains in bright nasturtium colors, heavy linen ones that could be drawn across the windows at night and give them the privacy the house lacked in the daytime. She had bought two pictures—the windows took up too much wall space for pictures to show to any advantage—and the kind of attractive modern china that went with the furnishings. She had said nothing at all about missing the old polished wood and delicate traditional designs of century-old Dresden and Royal Worcester china which she had been accustomed to. She hadn't, after all, craved for chintz and a fourposter bed. But, among many other things, Luke hadn't realized she had needed a transition period. She couldn't grow used to her new setting all at once.

Because everything was so utterly different. Even Luke ...

But in eight weeks things were beginning to take on a more familiar look, and she thought that if only Luke's eyes would lose that hardness that couldn't come from living in the too bright sun, although people said it did, she would be happy.

The sun was dazzling already. It streamed through the wide windows of the living-room, and quivered on the green river where the shabby boat, painted a faded khaki, rocked gently at anchor. The boat had been anchored there ever since Abby had arrived, and for weeks before that, Luke told her. An itinerant Australian, perhaps one of the old swagmen type who had taken to the water instead of the road, lived on it. He occasionally did odd jobs in the neighborhood, Luke said, when he would row ashore in his leaking dinghy early in the morning and back again at night. To Abby he was just a vague shape, pottering about his shabby domain, a scrawny figure usually dressed in nothing but a pair of faded denim trousers. But his odd jobs couldn't have amounted to much, for he always seemed to be there, playing records on his record player.

He was particularly addicted to one tune, a strident hit of the day.

The platypus was in a frightful fuss

7

When he met the roo . . .
Wouldn't it be fine to ask her to dine . . .
But I love only you-oo, I love only you . . .

The tune was rapidly becoming Abby's theme song to Australia. She did all her household chores to the thin wailing strains drifting across the slow-flowing river.

She hadn't yet got to the stage of unbearable irritation, but if Jock didn't soon tire of that tune, she would. Luke called the man Jock. He didn't know his real name. He said he had never met him. But there he was, day after day, always looking up towards the house, like a private eye watching.

'Well, you look down at him as much as he looks up at us,' Luke pointed out reasonably.

'It's just that he seems to stare.'

'Then draw the curtains.'

'I know I can. But I like to look at the river. It's cool. And if I have the curtains drawn this side, then I have Mrs. Moffatt or Milton looking down on the other. Or those beady-eyed kookaburras staring in. Or that little horror, Deirdre.'

'Granted you're decorative enough to look at, darling, I don't think all those people are that interested in what you're doing.'

'I don't suppose they are, but they have nothing else to do. That lazy creature on his boat, poor Milton stuck in a wheel chair.'

Luke laughed again. He wouldn't take her

8

seriously. 'Then give them a little pleasure.' He didn't realize that in even so short a space of time as eight weeks she was getting a fixation about being stared at. She must certainly try to hide such a silly state of mind from him.

Nevertheless it grew a little more each day. She drank her coffee to the thin strident music from the boat, *I love only you-oo, I love only you* . . . and then started violently as a movement at the window caught her eye. It was a flash of pink which disappeared as she turned. She sighed and waited.

Presently, as she had expected, the thin, foxy little face appeared, unashamed now that it was observed. The sharp nose pressed against the windowpane, the meagre body in the faded pink shirt and jeans stood in an attitude of expectancy. There was a tentative grin.

It was Deirdre, Lola's daughter. Abby thought she was the least attractive child she had ever seen. Because of that, she couldn't be unkind to the poor thing, although, as well as being unprepossessing to look at, she shared her family's inquisitive traits. In some uneasy way she reminded Abby of herself. She too had had a lonely childhood with a stepfather at an early age, and a mother who was too young and pretty and devoted to her own personal interests to give much time or understanding to the daughter of an early unhappy marriage.

Although she hadn't peered in windows as this child did, she knew all too well the feeling of being shut out, of looking in at other people's happiness as if there were always an impenetrable glass wall between them.

So she couldn't quite bring herself to be harsh to Deirdre, and the consequence was that the child seemed to be giving her an embarrassing devotion. This took the form of always lurking about, either appearing silently at the window, or scuffing dust in the garden, or perching on a rock half-way up the hillside and staring with the basilisk stare of the lizards. She had a thin, white face and tufted, sandy hair and eyelashes. She had almost no flesh over her small bones. She ate like a horse, her mother said, but where was the result? She took after her father in San Francisco. Or was it Singapore? Or the mountains of the moon? Although she went to school, she seemed to have no friends of her own age. She was a solitary, either from unpopularity or her own desire. One thing one would never know was what went on in her secretive mind.

But now she was tapping peremptorily at the window, some small object in her hand.

Reluctantly Abby went to the door and opened it.

'Hullo, Deirdre. Why aren't you at school?'

'It's a holiday.'

'Then why aren't you doing something more

10

interesting than looking in my windows?'

The child looked at her with simple honesty.

'What is there to do?'

'Well—I suppose your mother's at work.'

Deirdre shrugged.

'She said she might buy me a dress today if she had time.'

Deirdre's thin wrists usually stuck too far out of her school blouses, and the hemline of her tunic crept higher and higher up her growing legs. But Lola was always smartly dressed. She had to be, she said, in her job. You couldn't work in a smart beauty salon and look dowdy. Deirdre's father had apparently never been around since she was born. Whether Lola was entitled to be called Mrs. Henderson was a matter for conjecture. But she did say that, seeing what a plain baby Deirdre was, and thinking of the handicaps of bringing her up presumably more or less permanently without a father, she had at least given her a fetching name. It was something.

'That's nice, Deirdre,' Abby said. 'But in the meantime, what are you going to do all day?' (Although she was no longer a lonely child herself, she, too, was burdened with a too long, too empty day. There was this uncomfortable bond between the child and herself.)

'I don't know. Mooch around.' The child was deadpan. She didn't show she cared. 'Milton had a bad night, Mary says, so I'd better make myself scarce. Gran might let me

11

have her beads for a while. Only I broke a string last time, and she was wild. The amber ones. But we found them all. Mary says so long as I don't make a racket in the house.' Instinctively Deirdre looked over her shoulder towards the window where Milton might be sitting. 'I'll be glad when he's back in hospital,' she said flatly.

'Is he going back soon?'

'I guess so. It's about time. He hasn't been since last school holidays.'

Milton's trouble was obscure. Even Luke didn't know much about it. An accident which had damaged the spine, requiring frequent hospital treatment. Milton was not a man who cared to discuss his infirmity. He had a tense, irritable, heavily-browed, handsome face and an abrupt manner. Living with him must be like living with a live electric wire. No wonder Deirdre kept out of his way, and Mary, his wife, was meek and nervous and subdued. Quite unlike her sister Lola.

'Then you'd better go and see your grandmother, hadn't you?' Abby suggested. 'I have to get on with my work.'

'Yes. I guess so.' The child shuffled. Then suddenly her face brightened. She held out a tightly wrapped object.

'I almost forgot. I brought you a present.'

'Why, Deirdre! You shouldn't have done that.'

'Take it,' the child said impatiently. 'It's only

a lipstick.'

Abby unfolded the scrap of paper, disclosing the lipstick in its smart gold case.

'But this is new, Deirdre. Where did you get it?'

'Mummy's got dozens.'

'Dozens? Surely not.'

'Yes, she has. She gives them away. She gets them from work.'

'But I don't think—'

'Don't you want my present?' said Deirdre, deeply hurt.

'Of course. It's sweet of you. But would your mother—'

Deirdre waved her bony little hands.

'Oh, don't bother about her. She won't care.'

Then abruptly, with her peculiar ability to vanish silently, she had turned on her heel and disappeared round the house.

Abby shrugged. Lola's lipstick. She didn't want it, but she absently removed the top and looked at the color. It was a vivid pink, and was called Galah, presumably after the Australian parrots with the rosy underwings. So it must be a local product. Abby noticed a small curl of paper on the floor which must have slipped off the lipstick. She picked it up and read the printing 'Rose Bay Cosmetic Co.' Nothing more.

She twisted up the paper and threw it in the wastepaper basket. But the color of the lipstick was nice. She would use it tonight and wear her white shantung dress.

So far she had worn very little of her carefully selected trousseau. There hadn't been the opportunity. If one hadn't married Luke one might almost have said marriage could be rather dull. The short ceremony at a small modern church in a Sydney suburb, dinner at a rather dark very expensive restaurant called unromantically The Duckbilled Platypus, and then home. Luke had given her her choice of an hotel, or their own house, and she had unhesitatingly chosen the house. She had told herself that every newly-married couple should spend their first night in their future home.

She still stubbornly maintained this, although she had had her first startled awakening to the laughter of the kookaburras, and for a nightmarish moment she had thought that everything in this new strange country was mocking her, even Luke. For although he was laughing at her fright, there was that hardness in his eyes—as if he were all the time considering not her but something else. Or someone else . . .

And after that Luke had said he had to go to the office for a little while. On their very first day of married life! So she had been left to make the discovery of the elusive half-naked man in the boat on the river, who kept looking up, and of the Moffatts whom, of course, she had met previously but whose habit of looking out of their high windows down to her house she hadn't known. And of Deirdre's scarecrow shadow always lurking.

So there hadn't been much occasion to wear her honeymoon clothes. But she might have expected that, for she had come out from England against Luke's wishes. He had wanted to wait another year before they married. He had said he would be firmly established in his profession by then, but at present with all his financial commitments things would be tough.

Abby had preferred the toughness to the separation. She loved Luke so much. When she had met him in London two years previously he had been unrecognizably gay and light-hearted. Or unrecognizable from the way he was now. She had foolishly imagined their courtship would go on after marriage. She had thought the two years that had left her unchanged would have been the same for Luke. But she might have been warned by his letters. Wait, he had kept saying. He loved her, of course, but wait.

Was it really because of his stringent financial circumstances, a thing that hadn't bothered him too much as a bachelor, but seriously did as a husband and a home provider? Or was it because his older brother, Andrew, to whom he was deeply attached, was at present exploring in the wilds of Alaska and couldn't be at the wedding?

15

Or was it anything to do with Lola? Lola, the tall sunburnt Australian with the zany humor and the sun-bleached hair. Not the dark-haired soft-voiced English girl with whom he had had fun in London, but one of his own kind, reckless, high-spirited, not too overburdened with morals.

While still in England Abby had flatly refused to believe that Luke might really not have wanted her to come. As soon as they were together all would be well. She had only to remember Luke's blue eyes, so full of love, the hungry way he had held her and his promises that there would never be anyone else.

She had been twenty-four that spring, and life seemed to be flying by. To wait another year was crazy, when all that happiness was there to be taken. So she had refused to listen to her mother who had said that surely it was Luke's duty to come for his bride. She insisted that Luke needed his money for their home, and that it shouldn't be spent on unnecessary travelling. The practical thing was for her to go out to him.

So she had gone, without a doubt in her mind, and waiting on that rather dismal pier in Sydney's harbor eight weeks ago had been the hard-eyed stranger.

But he had married her. And that night he had buried his face in her hair and muttered, 'Try to understand, Abby. Try to understand.'

But what she had to understand, she hadn't the faintest idea, for after that they had been simply a man and a woman, and perhaps it was the pain and the ecstasy of her first loving that she had to understand.

All she knew was that it bound her to Luke forever . . .

The long day ended with the sun setting behind the monastery on the hill. The sky went shining pink, the cross over the monastery a slim pencilled black. The row of cypresses turned the scene sharply Italianate. There was a vague melancholy about this view from the big picture window in the living-room. Abby was more than ever conscious of it this evening, and longed for darkness so that she could draw the curtains.

She even turned with relief to the river to listen to the commonplace twang of Jock's gramophone. This new country kept making her feel disorientated. It was a mixture of too many things, old and new. It was going to take her a long time, even with Luke's help, to settle down.

But as darkness grew she became more cheerful. Luke would be home any moment now. She had prepared a small elaborate meal. She took a quick shower and changed into the white dress. Then she tried Lola's lipstick and found it an intriguing color with the dress. She tasted the slight rather pleasant flavor as she pressed her lips together. If Deirdre were to get into trouble about the gift to which she had obviously helped herself, Abby would have to defend her. But the color looked well against her clear skin. She brushed her short dark hair and smoothed her eyebrows. Her heart beat a little faster. Would Luke notice the lipstick? Or her? Would it make him emerge from his preoccupation, almost his obsession, about his work?

Once she had been his obsession. She would be again.

The determination made her light-hearted. When she heard Luke's car she ran to open the front door.

'Hi, darling! You're home early.'

Luke got out of the car, a tall man with powerful shoulders and a slim wiry body. Abby's heart gave its familiar leap of pleasure at the sight of him.

But a moment later it sank, as he went round to open the other door and Lola's long sinuous form emerged from the car. It was Lola who answered Abby's greeting.

'Hi there. Can I come in for a drink? Just five minutes. Then I've got to dash.'

Luke said belatedly, 'Hullo, darling.' He came to kiss her on the cheek. 'Had a nice day?'

Abby thought of the long slow hours now safely past.

'A lazy one. I did nothing except cook for you and the kookaburras.'

18

'I thought you hated the kookies,' said Lola.
'I think they're cute. They're even learning not to laugh at me.'

She slid her hand into Luke's as they went indoors. His fingers closed round hers. But the next moment he was saying, 'What will you drink, Lola? Your usual?'

'Thanks, Luke. Say, that crazy man does play his records a bit persistently down there. Doesn't it drive you mad, Abby?'

Nothing drives me mad in Australia. I love everything, Abby wanted to say. Even you hanging around here. As I suppose you've been doing for weeks and months before I came . . .

But Lola was decorative in her casual deadpan way. Her eyelashes were curled, her eyes heavily made up. Her skin was a smooth golden brown. The straight skirt and top showed her flat elegant body. Like Deirdre, she was exaggeratedly thin, but she had learned to use her thinness to advantage. She was half exotic, half the outdoor type that was necessarily Australian. A fascinating mixture.

'I sometimes wish he'd play another tune,' she said lightly.

'The platypus and the kangaroo. Do you know, that's exactly Mary and Milton.' Lola gave her deep husky laugh. 'Mary can look just as meek and silly as a duck, and Milton's a bad-tempered old roo, always wanting to jump at somebody. Always craning his neck to look

19

out of the window. Have you noticed, Abby?'

'Sometimes,' said Abby. And not only Milton, she wanted to add. Your mother, too, with her flat brown face and crinkled gray hair. She comes quietly, and she's always smiling. You never know what's she thinking. Or any of them for that matter, except perhaps Milton who was probably always thinking angrily and resentfully of his crippled body.

'Why wasn't Deirdre at school today?' she asked.

'It was a holiday. Has she been bothering you again?'

Because Deirdre was so unlikeable and defenceless, Abby said, 'Not bothering me. She looked lonely.'

'She won't play with the other kids. She isn't popular. She's a bad mixer, poor little wretch. Not like me.' Lola laughed again and looked at Luke. 'She needs her father,' she said, and suddenly she wasn't laughing. Her eyes remained on Luke. They had an odd significance.

Luke was busy pouring a drink. He didn't look up as he said, 'When is he coming home?'

'Goodness knows. I haven't heard from him for ages. He's no letter writer. Well, neither am I, for that matter.'

Her face was deadpan again. She shrugged.

'You might as well know, Abby, I haven't seen my old man for a long time. Deirdre doesn't even remember him. I keep up the

20

fiction that he's coming home one day, but I don't even know that I want him now, you know. I get along. Better than poor Mary with Milton underfoot, anyway.'

Abby didn't want to pursue the subject. By asking too many questions she might have discovered that Lola didn't have a husband at all. And somehow that was a discovery she would much rather not make. She preferred to subscribe to Lola's fiction.

But I love only you-oo . . . I love only you . . . floated through the window from the dark river. Luke clinked ice in a glass. He handed a drink to Abby and smiled at her. His eyes had their contained impersonal look. The words of the song hadn't entered his consciousness, or he wouldn't have continued to look like that, as if she also were merely a visitor for drinks.

Lola swallowed hers and sprang up.

'I must fly. I've got a date. I've got to change and see my child gets her supper.'

Fly in, fly out. No wonder Deirdre was lonely.

'Did you buy Deirdre her new dress?' Abby asked pointedly.

'Oh my God! I promised her that, didn't I? But I've had such a day, you wouldn't believe.' To give her her due, Lola looked upset. 'I'll tell her I'll pick her up early from school tomorrow and take her to choose it herself. That's if I can possibly make it. It depends on the mood the boss is in.' Lola sighed

21

exaggeratedly. 'Sometime I wonder how I keep sane. Abby, you don't know how lucky you are, just one uncomplicated man to take care of— or to take care of you. I have mother at me, Milton at me, Deirdre at me, the boss at me, a salary to earn, an old man somewhere who doesn't give a damn. Honestly, I'm torn in about eight pieces.'

'If you're ever in a jam I could meet Deirdre from school for you,' Abby heard herself saying.

'Oh, no! Abby, you are an angel. Isn't she, Luke? Would you really be nice to my little horror?'

'I haven't that much to do,' said Abby guardedly.

'It wouldn't be often,' said Lola. 'But sometimes I'm in a fizz. And I can't let her cross that main road alone. The traffic's appalling. Really, Luke, it's the nicest thing you could have done, marrying Abby.'

She came to kiss Abby on the cheek. She smelt strongly of a heavy expensive perfume.

'Must go. Good-bye, sweetie. 'Bye, Luke. Thanks for the lift. See you in the morning?'

'Eight thirty,' said Luke. 'Not a moment later.'

'God! Isn't Abby lucky, being able to sleep?'

She had gone. The house was suddenly very quiet. Luke looked at Abby.

'Another drink, darling?'

The first one had gone rather effectively to

22

her head. It must have been stronger than usual.

'Yes, please,' said Abby. She resented Lola bitterly, she was even a little afraid of her, but now she had gone there was too much silence. She must get back her gaiety. She waited all day for the evenings. If they were to become failures, too, what was to happen?

'Luke, is Lola's husband really in San Francisco?'

'So she says. Or thinks.'

'Did you ever meet him?'

'No. I've told you before that I haven't.'

'I know. I didn't mean quite that.' Abby sipped her new drink, and felt pleasantly vague. 'I suppose I mean have you met anyone who might have been Deirdre's father?'

Luke looked at her levelly.

'Your guess would be as good as mine, darling. I don't know Lola that well. I've only met the family since I bought this piece of land.'

This was what he said. But he specifically said 'the family', not Lola. She couldn't cross-examine him. She must be more subtle.

'Does Lola have a lot of men friends?' she said lightly.

'She's out a good deal, yes. She's a lively person. I expect that household is rather suffocating.'

'But she leaves her child in it.'

'I know. It's a difficult situation. By the way,

that was nice of you to say you'd help with the kid.'

Abby sighed.

'I detest that child, but I can't help feeling desperately sorry for her. I don't know how long I can put up with her haunting this place, but—oh, let's forget her. Is Lola to be the only person to kiss me tonight?'

Luke grinned and came towards her.

'Fair enough.'

His hands were pressing through the thin material of her dress. She closed her eyes, not wanting the shock of seeing that his had not softened—once, at the beginning, she had opened hers to see him bending over her with a speculative coldness, as if his thoughts were far from the urgency of his body—so now always she let his lips and his body tell her that he loved her.

I love only you . . . The thin bleating voice from the river died away, and Luke sprang back from her.

'Where did you get that lipstick?'

'Why—' He was rubbing his lips violently. 'Don't you like it?'

'I asked you where you got it?'

It had a distinctive flavor. She had noticed that when she had put it on. Now Luke recognized it. He recognized it as Lola's, of course.

'Deirdre gave it to me,' she said flatly.

Abruptly he handed her his handkerchief.

24

'Take it off. Every trace.'

'But, Luke! Why on earth—'

'I don't like it, that's why. And I don't like you accepting presents from that child. You might know she took it, anyway. Do you want to encourage a child to pinch from her mother?'

Abby was almost in tears.

'But Deirdre would have been so hurt. And I liked the color. I intended to tell Lola.'

Luke took the handkerchief back from her, and tilting her head up scrubbed at her lips himself.

'I don't want you to get too mixed up with that kid. It's one thing to do a good turn by meeting her from school, it's another to encourage her to hang around here all day, and take things from her.'

'I don't suppose it'll happen very often,' Abby said coldly.

'And now where's the lipstick itself?'

'On my dressing-table, of course.'

She watched Luke go to the bedroom. When he came back he went to the kitchen and opening the door of the rubbish shute threw the small gold object down.

It was only then that he began to look less tense and upset.

'There,' he said. 'Now I'll taste you. You, yourself.'

But his kiss on her pale lips was perfunctory. He was now only making a gesture . . .

CHAPTER TWO

When her mother came in Deirdre, bending over the stupid, old jigsaw puzzle that Uncle Milton had told her to do, made herself not look up. She looked beneath her lashes to the level of her mother's hands, and saw that they held nothing.

So she had forgotten the dress. You might have known she would. With tense fingers Deirdre silently broke a piece of the jigsaw in two. Then she did another, and another. When Uncle Milton discovered this, as he undoubtedly would, he would punish her. He was actually the only person she was afraid of, but this fact she would never allow him to discover. It would please him too much. Because he didn't like her any more than she did him. She was too active for him. He sat in his chair hating to see her thin, quick body moving wherever it pleased. Once he had been so irritated he had almost got up to pursue her. But he had heard Mary coming and had sunk back.

Of course he hadn't nearly got up because he couldn't. But it seemed as if his rage had lifted him. Mummy said you had to be sorry for him, but you couldn't be sorry for someone you didn't like. Mummy didn't like him much either, nor Gran. And Mary was scared of him.

So it was nice when he went to hospital.

'Well,' said Lola. 'Everyone here. Cosy.' She saw Deirdre and exclaimed,

'Oh, honey, I'm so sorry. I just didn't have time to look for that dress. It'll have to wait. You've got a birthday soon. Do you mind awfully?'

'No,' said Deirdre, not lifting her head.

'Lola, she was looking forward to that,' said Mary in her soft nervous voice. 'How could you have forgotten?'

'I told you, I just didn't have time,' Lola said irritatedly. 'It's all very well for you, staying home. You've no idea what my day's like. I'm whacked.'

She collapsed into a chair, stretching her long slim legs. Milton looked at her, saying nothing.

'Anyway, where's she going to wear it?' Lola went on. 'She won't go to parties. She's happier in those old jeans. Aren't you, hon?'

Mrs. Moffatt lifted her gray frizzled head from her work, a piece of gros point, very intricate and subtly colored.

'A little girl should have pretty dresses. Deirdre would like them well enough if she was encouraged to wear them. Wouldn't you, dear?'

'No,' said Deirdre, breaking another piece of the jigsaw.

'All right, all right, don't go on at me,' Lola said exasperatedly. 'She can have wardrobes of

27

them one day. So can her poor hard-working mother. Maybe sooner than we think. I've heard from—'

Milton made the merest movement, a shuffle in his chair, and Lola checked herself, saying,

'Deirdre, hon, it's time you were in bed.'

Deirdre, scuffing all the pieces of the puzzle into a heap, didn't answer.

'You gave her her supper, didn't you, Mother?'

'Yes, dear.' Mrs. Moffatt had a wrinkled, brown face that looked as if it had been exposed to the sun for years. Her liquid brown eyes were narrow, observant, anxious. She was a little like a lizard, with her wrinkled watchfulness. Several strings of brightly-colored beads hung round her scrawny neck. 'She had egg and cereal and fruit. When she came in, that is.'

'I suppose she was down at the Fearons' again.'

'Well—somewhere.'

'I have to be somewhere,' said Deirdre to herself.

Lola sat up brightly.

'You like Abby, don't you, pet?'

'She's all right.'

'She likes you, anyway. She says she'll get you from school on days when no one else can. You'll like that, won't you?'

'I must say that's kind of her,' said Mrs.

Moffatt. 'She seems a nice little thing.'

'Harmless,' said Mary.

'She's quite attractive,' said Lola fairly. 'English looking, of course. Wait and see what the sun does to her skin.'

'She shouldn't be encouraged too much,' said Milton suddenly. 'I told you from the beginning.'

'I don't agree,' said Lola. 'Better the devil you know—'

'She can be watched from a distance,' said Milton.

'Is Luke happy?' asked Mary in her soft voice.

'Happy? Well, I don't know.' Lola glanced round. 'Deirdre, I told you to go to bed.'

Deirdre stood up in a leisurely way. Her blouse had come untucked from her jeans. There were faint hollows of tiredness beneath her eyes. Her face was sharp and defiant.

'If you want to know,' she said deliberately, 'I gave Abby one of your lipsticks today.'

There was a complete silence in the room. They were all looking at her. Now they would say, 'Where did you get the lipstick? Did you steal it? Why did you steal it? Why did you want to give it to Abby Fearon?'

She answered the last question that hadn't yet been spoken.

'I gave it to her because I like her. Actually, she's my only friend.'

Still nobody spoke. Then suddenly her

mother said flatly, and not to Deirdre at all, 'Something will have to be done about that.'

'Send her to bed,' said Milton abruptly.

Deirdre tried to stare defiantly into his cold, gray eyes, too prominent, like Gran's pigeon-egg beads, but her own fell. Milton was the one who frightened her.

'Yes, you get to bed,' said Lola. 'And you stay home, in future. Abby doesn't want you hanging round all day. Now get upstairs. And go to bed. Don't sit mooning at the window.'

Deirdre obeyed slowly, her defiance not quite gone. When she reached her room she did go to the window and stand looking out for quite a long time. She thought the curtains might not be drawn in the house below, and she would be able to see Abby and Luke sitting at dinner.

But the curtains were drawn, showing no chink of light. The only light came from the boat lying down in the river. It shone on the tiny deck, and as Deirdre watched she saw the skinny man come out. He tipped something overboard out of a bucket, and then just stood doing nothing. She could see the faint, pale gleam of his face so that she knew he was looking up the hillside.

Presently he waved to somebody. In her interest to see who it was, Deirdre leaned so far out of her window that she nearly tumbled into the garden below. She could just see her mother standing on the veranda. And she was waving back. Why ever should she wave to that dirty old man? Deirdre both hated and feared him.

Then, quite clearly, Milton's voice came behind Mummy.

'How can you be so careless with your stuff? You know that child's a jackdaw. Always poking about and meddling.' His voice was that of an irritable old man.

'I know, I know. But is it so serious?'

'Of course it is.' Belatedly Milton added, 'The child's turning into a thief.'

'It's a pity she isn't a more mercenary type,' Lola was saying reflectively. 'And the other way—we'd lose Luke if we tried that.'

'Exactly what I said from the beginning. You girls get carried away by a handsome face.'

'We can't lose Luke!' said Lola.

'We'll see. Anyway, tell me what happened today. It was all right?'

'Fine— No trouble . . .'

Their voices faded away. Disappointedly Deirdre realized that she wasn't going to hear herself discussed further. Since there was nothing else to do, she got into bed. She hoped she would go to sleep quickly, and that nothing would wake her.

It was much later that she heard the walking up and down. She hadn't heard it so much lately, but it was one reason why she hated going to bed.

Obscurely it was so frightening. One, two,

31

three, four, five, six steps this way, a pause, and then six back. Measured, like a big clock ticking.

She didn't know why she thought it might be the man from the boat walking in their house. She had never told anybody that she heard these footsteps or that she was frightened. But one night she meant to be brave enough to tiptoe to the head of the stairs and look down and see who it was. So long as he didn't lift his strange face and see her. She had a feeling that something terrible would happen to her if she were seen.

She knew that the footsteps were those of a man because Lola and Mary both walked quickly on high heels, and Gran flip-flopped in slippers. And Milton couldn't walk at all. So if it wasn't the horrible man from the boat, who was it? Sometimes she wondered, crazily, if it were her father . . .

CHAPTER THREE

Abby saw the light go out in Mrs. Moffatt's room, which was next to Deirdre's on the top floor. Much later the one in the big bedroom on the ground floor which was Mary's and Milton's was extinguished. But one in the living-room stayed on very late. She had been asleep and woke some time in the early hours to see it still shining.

She hated this twenty-four hour long consciousness of her neighbors. But unless she and Luke wanted to suffocate in dark airlessness she had to draw back the curtain and open the windows after they had put their own light out. So that the first thing she saw when she opened her eyes in the morning was the big stone house towering over them.

It gave her vaguely the same feeling that the gigantic bridge over the harbor did, an overwhelming consciousness of some heavy shadow hanging over her. When she crossed the harbor in the ferry the cheerful chugging little boat ploughed easily through the sparkling blue water until it reached the bridge. Then the mass of steel girders was strangely nightmarish, and her skin prickled with chilliness as the sunlight momentarily vanished. The bridge hung at the end of every street in Sydney. One turned a corner, and there it was, curved against the sky, disproportionately large, making everything else seem shrunken.

Just as the Moffatts' house, built in the lavish days of the late nineteenth century, towered over hers and Luke's modest one. Just as the faces at the window looked down from a superior height at her . . .

But this was the last half of the twentieth century, and the world was too full, and one had to grow accustomed to being overlooked.

It was three o'clock in the morning. A time for strained imagination and morbid fancies. Abby shifted carefully, trying not to disturb Luke as she looked at the peaceful shape of his face. Instead of going away from her in sleep, he seemed closer. Nothing else tugged at his mind, and he lay quietly beside her, all hers.

*   *   *

In the morning Lola was at the door before they had finished breakfast.

In spite of her weary voice, she looked bright and energetic and attractive in a tan-colored suit and white gloves.

'Isn't this grim, getting up at the crack of dawn. Hi, Abby. Aren't you lucky, having the whole day to amuse yourself. I can't think what you're doing up at this hour.'

'My husband likes to eat,' said Abby. 'Have some coffee. Luke isn't ready yet.'

Luke sprang up, wiping his mouth with his napkin.

'Yes, I am. 'Bye, darling. Be good.'

With Lola's eyes on them, his kiss was again perfunctory. Was it time to tell Luke that she didn't much care for all this chauffeuring he was doing of Lola? But they were neighbors. It was a neighborly thing to do. Otherwise Lola would have the long bus or ferry ride into the city.

All the same, Luke might have asked what she planned to do today.

What did she plan? The housework, the shopping, the walk to the library to change her books, perhaps a visit to the hairdresser if she could get an appointment.

Suddenly Abby had a moment of panic, seeing her life stretching out aimlessly ahead. Luke, preoccupied with his work in the daytime, his thoughts in the evenings, Luke beside her asleep until dawn. And what else but these aimless hours ahead?

In London she had been madly busy running a small flat and doing a full-time job as assistant to the beauty editor on a magazine. As a result of that job she knew a great deal about cosmetics, probably more than Lola had begun to know.

It was a pity to waste that knowledge. Indeed, why should she? Alone in the now too quiet house Abby suddenly came to a decision. She would begin a series of articles on beauty treatment and sell them to one of the local newspapers or magazines. She wouldn't tell Luke what she was doing until she had got a market. If it came to that, why shouldn't she begin looking for a market at once. She could go into the city this afternoon, after spending the morning preparing a series of ideas. The accent would have to be on outdoor life, since every Australian spent nine months of the year in the sun, and a great deal of that time on beaches.

She could re-hash that article she had done about make-up and fashion on the Italian Riviera. And then do something on face lotions and perfumes. Perfumes . . . That reminded her of the intriguing taste Lola's lipstick had had. That was a gimmick that could well be explored, the flavor of lipstick, and its resulting tug at memory.

From the man's angle he could be nostalgically reminded of lost loves. Let's keep it light, gay, sophisticated, non-sentimental. Let's look at it the way she was making herself look at that little episode last night.

One of the kookaburras was at the window, staring at her with its beady, intense eyes. The other two sat on the clothes line, fluffing their feathers and looking cross.

'Okay, okay,' said Abby cheerfully. 'Breakfast coming up. Just don't start squawking for it.'

It was while she was on the patio feeding

the kookaburras that there was a knock at the back door. The birds flew up, startled. Abby smoothed her hair and went through the house to open the door.

A scrawny man dressed in faded denim trousers and a crumpled shirt stood there. He had thin, dark hair and a mass of wrinkles over his sunburnt face. His eyes were pale blue and ingratiating.

It was a moment before Abby realized that he must be the man off the boat, the man Luke called Jock, for want of a better name.

'Morning, missus,' he said in a flat nasal voice. 'Just wondered if you wanted any gardening done. Or any odd jobs. I live right down there on the river. Kind of convenient.'

Abby couldn't have explained why she had such a sudden dislike for the man. It must have been an accumulation of the irritation she had experienced from the constant noise of his record player.

'I'm sorry. Not at present, I'm afraid. We're planning to have our garden landscaped,' she felt it necessary to explain. 'So nothing can be done until then.'

'That's all right, lady. Just thought I'd ask.' The man was annoyingly cheerful. 'I'm right down there. You could give me a shout if you needed me. Your husband's away a lot, isn't he?'

'No,' said Abby coldly.

'Thought he was. I see his car go away.'

Was there no escape from the watching eyes? Abby felt a twinge of something that wasn't just irritation. It was apprehension, and the beginnings of fear.

She ignored the man's impertinent remark, and said coolly, 'But one thing, I do wish you'd play your records more quietly. I like music, too, but not necessarily yours, or all the time.'

The man's eyes narrowed. He gave a cackle of laughter.

'You don't like the platypus and the 'roo. I've kind of got that one on my mind. Sorry, lady. I'll tune her down.'

He shuffled off, and she closed the door, standing a moment against it. He didn't want work, her mind was telling her. He only wanted to see me. Or to tell me he was there, watching. So now I can never stop being aware of him . . .

But if she told Luke that fancy he would laugh at her. He would say, 'What, old Jock! That old scrounger! He's perfectly harmless.'

And perhaps he was. Perhaps her imagination was distorting things once again. It was because she was alone too much. All the more reason why today she must make a start on something that would take her out of the house and keep her busy. She would sit down and sketch out some ideas at once . . .

'Are you going to town?' called old Mrs. Moffatt as Abby went up the path round the big house to the street.

The wrinkled brown face with the curiously sad eyes leaned out of the downstairs window. Abby could see the old lady's smile. She was so eager to be friendly. Strings of gaily-colored beads hung round her neck. She decorated herself like a Christmas tree. She was both eager and forlorn, and one had the feeling that either she was acting, or else she really was, like Deirdre, lonely and shut out.

'I've got some shopping to do,' Abby called up to her. 'Isn't it a lovely day?'

'Are you going by ferry, dear?'

'Yes.'

'Then don't be late home. The ferries get so crowded later. Don't they, Milton?'

Abby had not imagined the movement at Mrs. Moffatt's side. But she couldn't see Milton clearly because he would be in his wheel chair.

'The traffic's terrible,' the anxious delaying voice followed Abby. 'We can't even let Deirdre come home from school alone. Yes, Milton. I'm sorry, Abby. Milton says I'm keeping you. Have a nice time.'

Abby hurried on, relieved to escape. The old lady was lonely. She was bullied by Milton and her daughters. She was garrulous and had no one to listen to her. But Abby was glad only to get away, to escape the watching eyes and the constant inquisitiveness. What had they all done before Luke had come here to build his house in their garden? Stared at the lizards?

My name is Abigail Fearon. I'm twenty-four and just married. My husband is a surveyor just beginning on his own, and working very hard. Naturally he has to be away a lot, and I get a lot of spare time. It would help me to settle down much more quickly if I had a job and met more people. I've only been in Australia eight weeks, but I think it's wonderful . . .

All the way to town on the ferry Abby rehearsed what she would say to the editor or editors whom she hoped would agree to see her. She had drafted out a list of ideas and projects. She was so optimistic about her scheme that she didn't even notice as they slid beneath the great chilly arch of steel suspended miraculously above the little ferry boat. Her eyes were on the opposite shore where Sydney's skyscrapers gleamed pale in the brilliant sunlight. As the water grew blue and sunlit again she even thought the bridge had a strange beauty, and it didn't give her that oppressive feeling any more.

On shore she caught a bus up to Kings Cross which was her first destination. She wore a red suit and a small black velvet hat, and looked, had she known it, very pretty indeed. She thought that when her own private business was over she might call at Luke's office and surprise him. Perhaps they could eat out that evening, and be gay. It was time they behaved like newly-married people.

The Cross was full of bustling people, and the rich heavy scent of flowers from the flower shops, carnations, stocks and great orange poppies, hung in the air. Rows of old houses with lacy iron balconies and paint-flaked walls, reminiscent of another era, faced tall blocks of luxury flats. Bird cages and twining plants hung from blackened ceilings. Abby paused, fascinated by the juxtaposition of wealth and poverty. It was then that the name caught her eye and made her look again.

The Rose Bay Cosmetic Company. Now why did that seem significant?

It was a very modest notice over a door that opened from the street between a dress shop and a jeweller's and led up a narrow stairway.

Abby paused again. Cosmetics were on her mind. That was why she had noticed the name.

No, it wasn't. In a flash the answer came to her. That had been the name on the paper round the lipstick Deirdre had given her yesterday. She had forgotten it because it hadn't been one of the giant companies. But now, like fate, she had stumbled on it. It was like fate indeed, for here was her opportunity to pursue the intriguing question of the lipstick flavor. She would go upstairs and present her credentials and ask precisely how the faint subtle flavor which her husband had unfortunately recognized had been put in the lipstick. It would make an excellent gimmick on which to base her first article.

Does your husband prefer to remember or forget that kiss?

Abby went briskly up the narrow stairs. They were uncarpeted and rather unswept, which suggested the Rose Bay Company was either very small and struggling, or very new. They were also dark and steep. This was an old building, probably built in the early days of Kings Cross, and its modernized façade didn't correspond with its interior.

At the top of the stairway there were only two doorways. One led into a washroom, as indicated by the faded white printing, and the other, a shabbily painted green door, told nothing at all.

Since there was no other door this was the one at which Abby knocked. She waited a few moments, listening for footsteps. It was dark and cool up here, after the heat of the sun in the street. The roar of the traffic seemed a long way off. The building was so silent, it might have been empty.

Nobody came to answer her knock. She knocked again, more loudly, and waited. Still no one came. Tentatively she tried the handle of the door, and found it locked.

Suddenly she felt as if she were trespassing on somebody's private premises. This was obviously not the business entrance to the Rose Bay Cosmetic Company at all. In any case, if it were called the Rose Bay Company, surely its premises would be at Rose Bay, that very attractive suburb of Sydney on the water front.

Disappointedly Abby turned away, and began to go down the stairs, her high heels tapping on the wooden treads. Then she found that she had dropped a glove outside the door, and had to go back to retrieve it.

It was as she stooped to pick it up that she heard the faint noise within the room, a curious furtive dragging sound.

It was at that moment, too, that the overwhelming feeling of being watched came over her again. There was an eye at the keyhole, she thought wildly. Or whether there was or not, there was certainly someone in the room.

Anger at this familiar suspicious pattern of sly watching took her boldly up to the door. She banged on it unceremoniously.

'I know there's someone in there. Open the door!'

Utter silence. The place was deserted, dead. Had she heard a sound? Or had it been noises from the street? She looked down the steep flight of stairs to the square of sunlight at the bottom. It looked so normal that her fancies seemed ridiculous.

She turned, meaning to give one last tentative knock, but instead gasped in shock.

The door had opened silently, no more than a few inches.

She found herself looking into a pair of

pale, red-rimmed eyes.

'You knocked. You want something?'

The voice was a flat monotone. Abby couldn't have said why she felt that first tremor of fear.

'I didn't know there was anybody there. I thought the place was empty.'

The man was showing a little more of himself now. He was meagrely built, and had a face curiously fishlike. A faintly gasping mouth, pale eyes, and hair so sparse over his skull that it seemed flesh-colored.

Not a pleasant individual, but simply a man, not a hobgoblin or a ghost. Abby pulled herself together, and asked more composedly,

'Is this the Rose Bay Cosmetic Company?'

'I don't know anything about that, lady.'

'But you must. The sign says so downstairs. What are you doing here if you don't know what place it is?' Determined not to be chilled by his flat stare, Abby worked herself into a state of indignation. Why was the door opened only that meagre six inches? What was in there, anyway?

A mad impulse made her give the door a sharp push.

'What are you hiding in there? Let me look. Either this is the Rose Bay Cosmetic Company or it isn't.'

Taken unawares the man had lost his grip of the door and it sprang open, to show a completely empty room except for some old

44

packing-cases in a corner that looked as if they had stood there for years.

There was another door at the side. It was opened the merest chink.

Again Abby had that chilling certainty that she was being watched.

A narrow, dirty window looked down into what must be a well, judging by the dimness of the light it gave. The sounds from the street were scarcely audible from here. The sunlight and the bustling normality might have been a thousand miles away.

The pale eyes of the man looked at her unblinkingly.

'I think you're in the wrong place, lady.'

'Then why is that notice up in the street?'

'Can't say. I'm only a workman.'

'Doing what?' Abby asked crisply.

'That wouldn't be your business, would it?' the man said, with deliberate insolence. 'If you want this Rose Bay Company, I can't help you. Sounds more like they'd be in Rose Bay. What did you want, anyway?'

'It was just to find out about a lipstick they make—'

That side door did move. She could have sworn it. What was she doing here, anyway, standing in an empty room asking a workman foolish questions about a lipstick? Something he couldn't have known about even had he been an employee of the mysterious Rose Bay Cosmetic Company. She was beginning to

45

babble. Because if she didn't that acute feeling of danger would take possession of her, and she wouldn't have known how to get herself out of this horrible room.

'It isn't really important. I'm sorry I disturbed you.'

'You've come to the wrong place,' said the man in his flat voice. 'I'd go—if I was you. For your own good.'

His words didn't necessarily hold a threat. The timbre of his voice hadn't changed. But Abby looked into his cold eyes and was galvanized into action. Muttering an apology, she was out of the room and running down the stairs. Running for that heavenly sweet sunlight. Not knowing why the dusty old packing-cases and the dirty window and the derelict room had filled her with such fear.

In the street she found herself trembling. What was wrong with her? The man had done nothing. It was she who had behaved idiotically, forcing her way into private premises. But in her mind's eye she saw the side door inching open, moving just that fraction. And contemplating who had been behind that frightened her even more than the strange, subtle antagonism of the fish-faced man.

Suddenly, in the bright noisy street, she felt terribly alone. It was not the first time she had felt very alone in this gigantic, alien country, but this time her solitude was something different—as if she were the one stranger among hostile people.

Of course she was imagining it. It all originated from Luke's behavior. If he had let her come really close to him she would never have begun thinking that everyone was hostile. But he hadn't, he was holding her away, so her feeling towards everybody was tinged with this hurt and suspicion.

Nevertheless, at this moment only Luke could comfort her, and with nothing but this thought in mind she made for the nearest telephone box.

Could she go up to his office and wait until he was ready to go home, she meant to ask. Because the thought of going home to the empty house with the kookaburras raucously screaming in the jacaranda tree, the thin strains of Jock's gramophone from the river, and Mrs. Moffatt calling to ask what she had done in town, were too much to contemplate.

Miss Atkinson, Luke's forty-year-old secretary, answered the telephone.

'I'm sorry, Mrs. Fearon. Mr. Fearon isn't in.'

'Oh!' Abby made a disappointed sound. She found that she kept glancing back down the street to see if the fish-faced man had emerged from the building. 'Will he be in soon? Can I come and wait? I'm in town and thought we might go home together?'

She made her voice light. Miss Atkinson was a matter-of-fact unimaginative sort of person, loyal to Luke but inclined to be bossy and managing. She had kindly but firmly made it clear from the start that she considered a wife's place was in the home, not hanging around her husband's business premises. Abby could have the new house by the river, but Miss Atkinson had the Elizabeth Street offices.

'Well, I am sorry, Mrs. Fearon, but he's gone out to Parramatta on a job. He said he'd be going home straight from there.'

'Oh!' Now the bottom had really fallen out of the day. 'Did he say how late he was likely to be?'

'He didn't say he'd be late at all.' Miss Atkinson's voice was brisk and reassuring. It told Abby not to fuss. It suggested that over-possessiveness could suffocate a man.

'Then—I guess I'll have to go home by ferry.'

'That's right. It's a nice day to be on the harbor. I wish I could be myself.'

All right, thought Abby crossly, don't lecture me. Don't think I'm a spoilt wife. Because you couldn't be further from the truth.

'You're all right, aren't you, Mrs. Fearon?' came the brisk, no-nonsense voice.

'Yes, I'm all right.'

'I thought for a minute you sounded nervous.'

Abby managed a laugh. 'What on earth about?'

'Yes, that's what I thought. In Sydney. Where are you ringing from?'

'The Cross.'

'Oh, well, odd things can happen up there. But not by daylight, usually. So don't be alarmed.'

Miss Atkinson was simply making conversation. She was relieved when Abby hung up, so that she could get back to her work. Real things, not the hypersensitive fancies of a spoilt bride.

But her attitude had done Abby good after all, for now she found herself quite calm enough to go into an espresso bar for coffee, and then to make the journey down to Circular Quay to catch the ferry.

There was a queue waiting for the ferry. She took her place and was jostled and hurried on board. Looking back as she found a seat she could not be sure, she could never be sure enough to tell it as a fact to Luke, but the figure sauntering behind the crowd which had just disembarked from another ferry looked remarkably like that of the fish-faced man. She could see his flesh-colored hair . . .

There were many middle-aged men with thinning hair which had gone that color. It would be so easy to make a mistake, and she had rather had him on her mind. But if it should have been him—and Abby's eyes strained after the vanishing figure as the ferry headed out towards the towering shape of the

49

bridge—there was only one conclusion she could draw. He had followed her to see where she went. Perhaps to satisfy himself as to who she was. Because he had more than half an idea already.

CHAPTER FOUR

Deirdre was hanging round the gate when Abby got home.

'Hullo,' she said. 'Are you wearing the lipstick I gave you?'

The subject of the lipstick had grown out of all proportion. Abby was very tired of it.

'Not today.' And then, because she couldn't hurt the child's feelings, she added, 'It's the wrong color for this suit. But I'm going to use it tonight. Did you tell your mother you took it?'

Deirdre shrugged. 'She doesn't care. She's got lots.'

'Where does she get them?'

'I don't know. From work, I guess.'

'Not from the Rose Bay Cosmetic Company?'

Deirdre swung on the gate. 'I don't know. Who are they? Can I come in with you?'

Beneath her blasé manner the child was desperately lonely. Abby knew that and made herself be kind.

'For ten minutes, then I have to start getting dinner. Would you like a cold orange drink?'

'I'd rather have lime,' said Deirdre unenthusiastically. 'Do you know, someone walks in our house at night.'

'Who?'

'I don't know. I'm scared to go and look. I think it's that old man off the boat.'

'Jock! What would he be doing in your house?'

Abby laughed incredulously. She had to laugh so that she didn't let Deirdre notice how that strange fear had pricked her again.

'I dunno.' Deirdre kicked pebbles with her scuffed shoes. Her confidence had been rare, and she had been afraid she might be laughed at. 'But it's a man, and there's no one else, is there? Uncle Milton can't walk.'

For no reason whatever, Abby thought of Luke lying quietly beside her, deep in sleep, while the moon rode over the bright sky.

Suddenly she put her arm around Deirdre's meager body.

'Silly girl. You imagine things just like I do. I even thought I was being followed home. I watch television too much. I expect you do, too.'

'It bores me,' said Deirdre cynically. 'We only have it because of Uncle Milton.'

'Well, goodness,' said Abby. 'Isn't it time you were eight years old instead of eighty?'

*　　　*　　　*

But it was she who was eighty when Luke was late. It had long since grown dark, and she sat in the quiet house listening. She didn't know why she listened so intently, for there was no

52

sound but that made by a night beetle bumping drunkenly about the room. What did she expect to happen? Jock had come this morning asking for work, and this afternoon she had blundered into someone's private premises. Neither of these things should give her such a queer feeling of oppression. But they did. When the telephone rang she started violently.

Then she sprang up, thinking it would be Luke.

The voice that spoke was a strange one, almost high-pitched enough to be a woman's, though with a queer certainty Abby knew it belonged to a man.

'Is that the little lady in red?' it said, with a snigger.

Abby stiffened.

'You have the wrong number,' she said coldly, somehow managing to speak without a tremor.

'Right number, I think,' said the voice laconically, and there was a click as the receiver was put down.

When the telephone rang again a few moments later Abby was still standing beside it. Tense with shock, the abrupt noise made her jump again. Who was it this time? Luke, surely. Not the fish-faced man playing a joke on her. For she had a quite unaccountable certainty that her previous caller had been the fish-faced man checking where she lived. He had somehow followed her all the way home . . . Or far enough to be nearly sure who she was.

But this time it was Lola wanting to know if she and Luke would come up for coffee and drinks that evening.

She pulled herself together and spoke normally.

'I don't know, Lola. Luke isn't home yet. He had to go to Parramatta.'

'I know that, the skunk. I had to come home by ferry. But he won't be late, will he? Do come.' She lowered her voice. 'You'll be doing us a good turn. Milton's in one of his moods and poor Mary has had it.'

'Can I give you a ring when Luke gets home?'

'Sure. What have you been doing with yourself today? Mother says you went into town.'

The grapevine again. Abby was determined not to be annoyed by neighborly interest. And it was such a relief to talk to someone. She had been bottling up tension for too long.

'Yes, I did go to town, up to the Cross. Lola, do you know what make that lipstick was that Deirdre gave me?'

'Haven't a clue, sweetie. I don't know which she took. We buy from various companies. I'm the guinea pig and try them out. Anyway, can't you look?'

Lola didn't know the lipstick was buried in

54

trash and ashes far beyond salvage, and Abby had no intention of telling her something that was private between herself and Luke.

'It had a bit of paper wrapped round it which unfortunately I've thrown away.' (She had searched in the wastepaper basket, but found she had emptied it that morning.) 'I'm sure the name of the company was the Rose Bay Cosmetic Company. Anyway, it rang a bell when I saw its sign in the Cross today, so I went in to have a look. But there was only an empty room, and a rather horrible man who threatened me.'

'Goodness!' said Lola. 'How queer! Have you told Luke?'

'I haven't seen him yet.'

'Well, I'd tell him as soon as he gets home. He'll warn you about going into strange buildings in the Cross. What made you go searching for this Rose Bay outfit, anyway?'

'I didn't go searching for it. I just happened to see the sign. I used to write articles on beauty and cosmetics in London. I planned to do some here to fill in the time. Then I thought up this lipstick gimmick—'

A hand was laid on her shoulder.

'What lipstick gimmick?' said Luke.

Abby gasped. She heard Lola's voice saying sharply, 'What's wrong?' (Almost, Abby thought afterwards, as if she had expected something to be wrong.)

Abby managed to laugh.

'Luke has just scared the wits out of me. I didn't hear him come in. Luke, Lola wants us to go up for coffee later.'

'Okay,' said Luke.

Why didn't he say he was too tired or too busy? Or make any excuse that would show he only wanted to spend the evening alone with his wife. But he was watching her, too, and it wasn't with the pleasure of being home in her company again. It was with speculation. But perhaps the shock she had just had still showed in her face. She hadn't got round to telling Lola the strange sequel to her visit to the Cross.

After saying to Lola that they would come, Abby put the receiver down, and said, 'Why are you staring at me like that?'

'What did you tell Lola about that damn lipstick? Are you upset because I wouldn't let you use it?'

Abby ignored the tone of his voice, and let her own troubles tumble out.

'Luke, I've just had the oddest phone call. One of those horrible anonymous ones, but the man must have known who I was because he called me "the little lady in red". And it's true, I did wear my red suit today.'

Luke's face changed. 'Tell me what happened,' he said curtly. 'Start at the beginning. Where did you wear your red suit?'

He listened intently while Abby related the story once more, this time completing it with

56

the telephone call and her certainty that her caller had been the fish-faced man.

'He either guessed who I was from the beginning, or else he did follow me home. Although I was sure he didn't get on the ferry.'

Luke regarded her intently, his eyes dark with thought. But all he said, rather irrelevantly, was,

'That innocent lipstick is having repercussions it doesn't deserve. So what if you did like the flavor. I didn't know women were accustomed to eating their lipstick. And why didn't you tell me you were thinking of doing this job? Wasn't I entitled to know?'

'I wanted to surprise you. And—'

'And what?' he asked, as she paused.

'Luke, don't mind my saying this. But you've been so absorbed in your own work and sometimes I wonder if you ever think about what I do all day. That wretched man on his boat gets on my nerves. And Deirdre hangs around, and I don't really know any people except the Moffatts. I—I guess I was just lonely.'

'And I didn't notice,' Luke finished. 'So you've begun to grow morbid, imagining people are watching you and following you.'

'I didn't imagine that man today,' Abby said sharply. 'He told me to get out for my own good. Why should he say that unless he was up to something suspicious? Why should he follow me? Have I seen something I shouldn't have? Luke, am I going to be haunted by that unsavory character? Just to see I don't poke my nose in again?'

Luke got up and went to the sideboard to pour a drink. He handed Abby a strong whisky.

'Drink that. You look as if you need it. And don't jump to conclusions. That's a very feminine characteristic. Yes, I know you've had a disturbing call, but why think it was that fellow, the fish-faced man as you call him? Couldn't it have been anyone who saw you go up the hill in your red suit? After all, you're worth looking at, my darling.'

Luke's attempt at lightness was not particularly successful. His face was still bleak.

'And from this minute, Abby, you're to get over this complex of being watched. I had no idea you felt like this. I know old Jock is a bit of a nuisance, but we can't do anything about that. The river's free, and he's entitled to play his gramophone. As for the Moffatts, they like you. They genuinely want to be friends.'

'Lola, too?' Abby said involuntarily.

Luke gave her a quick glance under tightened brows.

'Lola, too. She's a nice girl who's had bad luck.'

'You mean she doesn't have a husband at all? This is only a story for Deirdre's sake?'

'I don't mean that at all. As far as I know, Lola's husband is in the States. Whether he

58

comes back or not isn't our business, but I do believe he exists. So put that thought out of your mind.'

'I wouldn't dislike Lola because of that,' Abby murmured.

She saw that the precious sympathy had gone out of his face, and added bleakly, 'I guess I just don't feel much in common with Australians yet. You've had much longer at it than me, remember?'

'If you're going to generalize, we can't talk about Lola. So would you like me to say that she means nothing to me but a pleasant and amusing neighbor?'

'Luke, how did we get into this discussion?' Abby asked unhappily.

'I suppose via the lipstick, once more. Look, let's settle this business once and for all. I didn't want you to use that lipstick because it belonged to another woman, and I prefer you to have your own. Understand? It could have been any woman's, not particularly Lola's. And as for your little adventure today, we'll get that straightened out, too. Tomorrow you shall take me to this place and we'll find this man and settle his hash. If he has been making mischievous phone calls it can be a police matter. But we'll intimidate him a bit first.' He looked at her with his level gaze. 'All right?'

Abby nodded helplessly. Somewhere along the way of this discussion they had lost their closeness again. She didn't know where it had happened. With the mention of Lola, probably. After all, who else?

'You think I'm just being neurotic,' she said.

He frowned impatiently.

'Darling, please. I'm only trying to get this thing straightened out. It's all my fault, anyway. I should have realized you were lonely and bored. Perhaps it's a good idea that you do get a job.'

'Yes.' Abby swallowed the rest of her drink. It hadn't helped her to relax in the least. She didn't see how going back to Kings Cross and climbing those dark, grimy stairs again could help, either. Perhaps it was as well they were going to the Moffatts' for coffee. At least it would pass the evening.

The evening which she had waited for all day, she thought painfully, and sprang up before tears could come into her eyes.

'I'd better get the dinner if we're going out. Have you had a busy day? Miss Atkinson told me you'd gone to Parramatta.'

'Yes. It's a good job, too. You might even congratulate me.' He smiled, asking for her interest. As if she were a stranger. 'How did you come to be talking to Miss Atkinson?'

'Oh, I thought I'd wait in town and come home with you. I was a bit upset, I know. It was silly making that man open the door and getting into that place. I really asked for it. It was his face that frightened me most. It wasn't really evil, it was just—' she stopped, trying to think how to describe that flaccid, stupid, yet crafty face. 'After all, I don't much care for Jock, either. He came this morning asking for work. But he isn't really frightening like this other one. You must be right, Luke. I do have a complex. Perhaps I'm starting a baby.'

He came to stand behind her at the table and kiss her neck.

'Darling! I love you so much. Believe me!'

She didn't turn lest she destroy the precious unbelievable moment.

'Really?'

'Look at me!'

Then she had to turn, and immediately was sorry. She hadn't wanted to see such intense anxiety in his face.

'Luke, you really are worried about this.'

'Anything that worries you worries me. Don't be so stupid!'

Abby had to say something quickly to lighten the moment. What was wrong with Luke and herself? They were being so intense.

'I don't think I am starting a baby,' she confessed. 'It would be nice and rather old-fashioned if I were. Wouldn't it? I mean, so soon.'

She resolutely pushed the vision of Deirdre's thin sharp inquisitive and unlikeable face out of her mind. A baby needed a great deal, including loving and united parents. Poor Deirdre was to be pitied. Her own baby would

61

be happy and fortunate. Because Luke did love her after all . . .

CHAPTER FIVE

She had known exactly what it would be like in the Moffatts' living-room, a large high-ceilinged room with a cavernous stone fireplace that was never used, elaborate gas brackets and heavy Victorian furniture that had been used in the earlier days of Australian history.

Mrs. Moffatt presided over this. In spite of her anxious friendliness and her jumpiness, she was very much the mistress of her own house. Neither of her daughters could enjoy the old-fashioned furniture or the Victorian atmosphere, for both Lola and Mary were unlucky, one whose husband never came home and the other whose husband was an invalid.

So on the nights that Lola stayed in the scene must always be like this, the old lady in her high-necked black dress decorated with too many strings of beads, sitting alertly in the wing chair by the window, apparently busy with the multi-colored wools of her gros point, but missing nothing. Milton in his wheel chair, looking into space, until some irritation provoked one of his sharp outbursts, Mary at his side, pale-faced, subdued, rarely speaking, and Lola the restless one, not in the least intimidated by the oppressive atmosphere, turning on the radio too loud, talking incessantly, laughing.

There was no doubt that Lola was seen to great advantage when contrasted with her family. One had to admire her sheer vitality.

It was also not surprising that Luke had been a welcome and frequent visitor. They all, Lola particularly, must have regarded him as heaven-sent. But had he really only known the Moffatts since he had bought their piece of land six months ago and built his house? Were they, or Lola anyway, someone out of his past? Abby never knew why this thought niggled at her, but there was some element beneath the mere polite friendliness of neighbors. She wished she could ignore it or at least understand it. It didn't seem as if Luke would ever tell her.

Mrs. Moffatt asked Abby to come and sit beside her.

'Did you have a nice afternoon shopping, dear?'

'Actually I didn't shop.'

'Just window shopped. How wise. Think carefully before you spend, I always told my girls.' The brilliant brown eyes, slitted between their wrinkled lids, peered at Abby. 'You're looking so pretty tonight. But you English girls have beautiful skins. Not dried up with the sun like ours. Deirdre said you were going to use her lipstick tonight. How thoughtful of you, dear. You're very kind to Deirdre.'

Abby felt Mrs. Moffatt's eyes on her lips.

Not wanting to hurt the old lady's feeling by telling her that Luke had thrown the lipstick away, she just smiled, and wondered again whether she was ever going to hear the last of that tiresome present.

'Lola brings home so much muck from work. I'm sorry, I always call it muck. We didn't use cosmetics like this in our day. But naturally they have to try out new things before recommending them to their customers. Mary thinks Lola is lucky being free to go to work. She's so tied to Milton. And now there's this hospital treatment coming up again. It makes him so edgy, poor dear. He only puts up with it because he refuses to believe he won't walk again.'

The voice went on in its monotone, heard only by Abby, for the room was large and at the other end of it Lola and Luke were trying out a record on the gramophone. They were bending over it discussing it—or something else. Mary was pouring coffee, and Milton was looking at the ceiling, his narrow hands gripped together, his stone gray eyes as prominent as marbles.

'Elizabeth Street is a handsome street, isn't it? And now all those skyscrapers going up. Oh, yes, it's the country for young energetic people like yourselves. You won't be sorry you came. I was born here, of course. This was my parents' house. It used to be a fashionable area, but it's come down in the world. Like us,

I'm afraid. My father made bad investments, and then my husband died when he was quite a young man. I've brought up the girls as best I could.'

The music had abruptly come to an end, and in the moment of silence Abby heard Luke saying, 'I'm sorry I can't help more,' and stopping abruptly as he realized the silence.

Lola patted his arm.

'You've done enough for us already, honey. Just being around helps.' She turned to Milton to say, 'I've just been telling Luke you're due back in hospital next week.'

'I don't want help,' said Milton edgily. 'I can manage for myself. And don't think I'm in this chair forever. I'll walk again.'

'Of course you will, darling,' Mary's voice was gentle and comforting. But the coffee cup she was holding rattled in its saucer, and she gave a small exasperated exclamation. 'Oh, dear, I've spilt this. Lola, get a cloth.'

'Can't you do anything properly?' demanded Milton. 'Here I have to sit and watch you fumbling and bumbling.'

Mary's pale cheeks went even paler. Lola said in her aggressive way,

'Cut it out, Milt. It was an accident. And no wonder. You make her nervous, watching like that. Why don't you throw something at him, Mary?'

But she crossed over and pressed Milton's shoulder and the tension went out of his face.

Abby tried to feel genuine sympathy, but it was not easy with someone who was so difficult to like. Milton's intolerant eyes glared at everyone, even his wife. Most of all his timid subdued wife.

Luke had come to sit by Mrs. Moffatt.

'Did Abby tell you about her adventure today, Mrs. Moffatt? She thinks the Cross is a sinister place. I'm taking her back tomorrow to show her it isn't.'

'But it can be sinister, Luke.' Mrs. Moffatt was preparing to enjoy this promising conversation. 'There are so many strange characters up there today. And there's great wealth and great poverty, so things must happen. That's human nature, isn't it? But what did happen to Abby?'

Before Abby could reply, Mary had brought the coffee, and Lola had put another record on the gramophone. Milton said petulantly, 'Instead of all that noisy stuff, Lola, can we simply be old-fashioned and have the weather and the news?'

'Sure, Milt. Coming up.'

'Sugar?' Mary asked Abby.

'No, thank you.'

'No coffee for me,' said Mrs. Moffatt. 'It keeps me awake. Are you a television fan, Abby? Oh, it's a time filler, of course. But to me it's just retreating into a fantasy world. In my young days we were made to fill in time with constructive things. Needlework, if nothing else, and conversation. Informed conversation. We didn't go about the city alone, either, but I expect we missed a lot of fun.'

'Be quiet!' said Milton suddenly.

Mrs. Moffatt looked up in surprise. 'Sorry, Milton. I didn't realize you were listening to the news. Is there something particular—'

The impersonal voice of the announcer continued calmly,

'. . . is thought to have tried to swim ashore from the *China Star* which came in from Singapore this morning. The captain says he must have been a stowaway making a desperate bid to enter Australia. It will be remembered that some months ago a similar incident—'

Milton had snapped off the set.

'Only a Chink,' he said dismissing the matter.

'But nasty,' said Mary in her soft distressed voice. 'Poor man.'

Milton looked across to Abby, politely making an explanation.

'You may not know that Australia has pretty strict immigration laws. But from time to time some desperate Chinese or Japanese stows away on a ship and tries to swim ashore. Or else he dies on board ship, perhaps from suffocation in some locker, or from starvation, and his friends dump him overboard. Anyway, it isn't uncommon to find a body floating in

68

Sydney harbor.'

'That other one was white,' said Mrs. Moffatt, re-threading her needle.

'He was never identified. Some bum from the East, probably.' Milton took his coffee from Mary and said more amicably, 'I'm sorry about that grisly bit of news. I only wanted to hear world affairs. What do you think of Mr. K's latest, Luke?'

Luke jerked himself back to attention. It was so obvious that everyone looked at him.

'Afraid I haven't been following it too closely lately.'

'Lucky devil, you've got enough affairs of your own.'

'I wonder if he had a wife and a horde of children at home,' Mrs. Moffatt was saying with detached interest. 'They say Chinese do. And now there'll be the problem of his family wanting to bury him with his ancestors. He must have badly wanted to get into Australia if he was prepared to risk the sharks. You have to be sorry for these people. They say Australia is the oldest continent in the world, but is it meant just for the white man?'

'Don't forget the aborigines, mother,' said Lola. 'And you go up to the Cross if you want to see different colored skins. All the Chinese haven't been squeezed out.'

Luke stood up.

'Abby, it's time we went.' He looked round the room. 'Sorry, but Abby and I've had a busy day, and I expect you people have, too.'

He was almost curt. But he did look tired. He wasn't inventing an excuse. And Abby was more than ready to go. The Moffatts were kind, but not the easiest or the most fun-loving people in the world. There were too many under-currents. And the fragment of human tragedy hadn't helped with the gaiety. But at least it had prevented more discussion about that tiresome and trivial subject, the lipstick, which even Luke now seemed to have forgotten.

They walked down the slope in the fresh night air. Luke had left the light over the front door switched on, so that it wasn't too difficult following the path. All the same the night seemed strangely dark. Something seemed different.

It wasn't until Abby reached the door that she realized what it was.

'Luke! The boat's gone. Jock's gone.'

It was true, for not only was the yellow square of light from his cabin window missing, but the dark shape of the boat had vanished, and the river was empty.

'What a relief!' Abby exclaimed. 'Listen to that heavenly stillness. No gramophone. Honestly, that tune of his was driving me up the wall. And I forgot to tell you, he called here today asking for work. I don't know whether I'm too suspicious, but he really isn't the type of man I want about. He sounds too

70

deliberately servile.'

'I'm sorry he worried you that much,' said Luke. 'But don't be too optimistic. He'll probably be back.'

'Doesn't the swagman type move on periodically?'

'And comes back to his old haunts,' Luke pointed out.

However, Abby felt disproportionately light-hearted. They were stuck with the Moffatts as neighbors, but an itinerant boatman wasn't there forever.

It was a pity that she couldn't spread her light-heartedness to Luke. All at once he just seemed too tired. His face was drawn and there was a look in his eyes that might almost have been tormented. Abby said anxiously,

'Luke, aren't you feeling well?'

'I'm all right. Just tired. I've had quite a day.

'Then why did you say we'd go to the Moffatts?'

'I suppose I feel a bit sorry for them. They've got their tragedy, too, with Milton.'

'Too?' said Abby. 'Who else has?'

'I was just thinking of that poor devil fished out of the harbor. So far from home. He'd come all this way to die.'

'Luke, how sweet of you to be upset about that. Milton wasn't. He said it was just another Chink. But do these orientals think Australia is a paradise that they'll risk the sharks to get ashore?'

'Men do desperate things for private reasons,' Luke said slowly. 'Sometimes you don't know which is worst, physical danger or mental hell.'

'What are you talking about?' Abby asked uneasily.

He attempted to laugh. Suddenly he put his arms round her.

'Forget it, sweetie.'

'But that didn't sound like you. It sounded much more like your brother Andrew. Do you remember that night in my flat when Andrew went on and on about the color question? And we weren't in the mood for intellectual discussions. But I adore him, all the same. I wish he could have been at our wedding.'

'So do I.'

'Have you heard from him lately? Is he really in Alaska?'

'He wanted to write about the primitive life,' Luke said. 'He was always harking back to the simple state. Twentieth-century civilization had got itself into such a snazzle of complications, he said. He had this dream of trying to find out if a man's heart could still be a spiritual thing, or just the engine of a machine. He was always talking about that. You remember?'

'Yes,' said Abby quietly.

Luke's face was at last beginning to relax. It always did when he talked of the older brother for whom he had so much love and respect, and who had looked after him since their teens when they had been suddenly orphaned. Andrew was all he had before he had met her, Luke had told Abby.

'At last he'll have an excuse to grow that beard he hankered for,' Abby said. 'I'll bet it's an enormous one. But I wish he would write. How long is it since you heard from him?'

'About six months. I don't expect there's a very frequent post on the icecap.'

Abby giggled.

'I can see a postman in a red uniform struggling through the snow—'

Red . . . She hadn't escaped so far from the present after all.

'I should have worn a cotton dress today,' she said miserably. 'It was warm enough.'

'Abby, you're to stop thinking of that! I know things haven't been amusing today. But don't hold it against Australia. Or me.'

'Or you!'

'For leaving you to cope alone.'

'But you couldn't know what I was getting into. It was one of my less predictable moments. Don't you remember, you always said I was unpredictable?'

He smiled at last.

'And so you are. Tomorrow we'll get to the bottom of this affair. Trust me?'

'Oh, Luke! Of course.'

They were close again. As he kissed her, first gently and then with a growing desire that almost had a desperation, as if this physical thing between them were the only real one, Abby caught his excitement and pushed away her disquiet.

It was only afterwards the thought came to her that Luke made love as if he were trying to exorcize ghosts. What ghosts? What was it that she no longer knew about him?

In the first hint of daylight Abby awoke to a faint chug-chugging on the river. Her heart sank. She knew with certainty what that sound was. It was Jock coming back in his old disreputable boat, from whatever jaunt he had made. At the same moment a pale square of light in the Moffatt house was extinguished.

Did it seem like a coincidence?

CHAPTER SIX

The bright sky arched over the sun bleached hills, the pointed cypresses and gum trees, and the conglomeration of buildings that scattered over the low hills down to the water's edge. The bridge arched over the water and hung in a dark curve at the end of every street. As Luke swung the car round corners it was temporarily lost, only to appear triumphantly again, a threatening rainbow against the peaceful sky.

Abby sat in the middle between Luke and Lola. As they had driven out of the gate the kookaburras had suddenly burst into a loud, 'Haw, haw haw, ha ha ha!' which may have been indignation because of their missed breakfast, or in some mysterious way derisive, as if they knew the meaning of this journey in the early morning.

Lola talked all the way, simply because she was never silent. Luke made non-committal rejoinders. He had a look of hard purpose this morning. This was beginning to be his most familiar side. Abby wondered if moments like last night would grow fewer and fewer as he developed into the dedicated business man which so many men in this thriving city seemed to be. She said nothing at all, as Lola's chatter flowed over her head, and scarcely listened to it until she realized that she was being addressed.

'You mustn't think Milt's too cranky, Abby. You should have seen him before his accident. He was like Luke, keen and energetic and on the ball. Luke, couldn't we give him some fun before he goes into hospital next week? You know, he used to love going out on a kangaroo shoot. Look, why don't we arrange one this weekend?'

'Could he travel that far?' Luke asked.

'Oh, yes, he doesn't mind hours in a car. After all, he's got to sit wherever he is, doesn't he? We could take two cars.'

'I don't think Abby would care for it,' said Luke.

'It would be a chance for her to see the outback. But I agree, it's pretty primitive, and an English girl isn't used to that sort of thing. Have you ever gone shooting, Abby?'

'Quite frankly,' said Abby, 'I'd loathe to shoot a kangaroo, or to see one shot.'

'Well, they have to be, you know. They're pests,' said Lola cheerfully. 'All the same, it's a thought, Luke. Let's see what can be done. Abby could come up and stay with mother if she didn't want to be left alone.'

Luke turned to give Abby a quick glance. There was a strange gleam in his eyes. It looked like excitement. He wanted to go on this expedition. He also wanted her to stay at home. So was it the kangaroos or a week-end with Lola that was the attraction?

Last night he had said, 'Trust me?' and she had at that moment. But now it was the hard bright day, and he was no longer wakened by love. And they were just coming along the approach to the bridge. Luke slowed down to pay the toll, then they swept on to the smooth roadway, travelling fast, the huge steel arches above them.

'Would you mind if we arranged this expedition?' Luke was asking her.

Involuntarily Abby shivered.

'Are you worrying about the roos?'

'No, I always feel cold on this bridge.'

Lola gaped at her.

'Goodness, you are funny. We're proud of it. Aren't we, Luke. If you want a really sinister place, Abby, you'd better see the Gap. Just jagged cliffs and the sea miles below. You ought to take her there, Luke, if you want to give her a thrill. You must be a sensitive person, Abby. I mean, even this man yesterday telling you to clear off simply because you were in the way, I expect, gave you the jitters. You're just not used to our lack of manners.'

'It wasn't my suggestion to go back to that place,' Abby pointed out. 'I'd be very happy never to set eyes on that man again.'

'But if you've got this idea he's going to persecute you, Luke's quite right. It's got to be cleared up. Personally . . .' Lola stopped and Abby said coldly,

'Personally what? You think I imagined it?'

'No, I just think you read more into it than there really was. Don't you, Luke?'

Luke was looking straight ahead, watching the road. His jaw seemed to have hardened.

'We'll soon see,' he said non-committally.

'You both seem to have forgotten that there was also the telephone call,' Abby reminded them.

'A joke, probably,' Lola said. 'Our zany sense of humor. It may have been old Jock from the boat. He's a bit ga ga. Paying you out for not giving him a job.'

'How did you know he had asked for a job?' Abby said evenly.

'Mother saw him go to your door. She said old Jock was at his tricks again.'

'Tricks?'

'He works just long enough to buy beer.'

Luke's voice broke into their conversation.

'We'll be at the Cross in a few minutes, Abby. Watch carefully and see if you can spot the street. You said you didn't notice its name.'

'No, but I'm sure I'll recognize it. Drive slowly.'

'Not too slowly,' said Lola. 'I've got to be at work in fifteen minutes.'

They edged along the busy streets, alive and noisy with people going to work. Abby glimpsed a flower stall, brilliant with carnations and the great orange poppies.

'Near here, I think. Yes, it is. There's the

house with the birdcage on the balcony. It was round that corner.'

But the street into which they drove had no sign of any cosmetic company.

'It should be about here,' Abby said bewilderedly. 'It was next to a jeweller's shop. That looks like the shop there. No, it can't be,' she added disappointedly. 'There's no sign up. But I'm sure this is the street.'

'Lots of people have birds in cages up here,' said Lola. 'That must have been the wrong house on the wrong corner.'

'But I'm sure it wasn't. I remember the rubber plants, too. Let's go back there, Luke, and get out and walk. I'll find it more easily if I'm walking.'

'It might be miles,' Lola protested.

Luke swung the car round and went back to the top of the street.

'Let's do as Abby suggests.'

He parked the car and as Abby got out she was sure the birdcage on the rusty iron balcony was the one she had noticed yesterday. There was a canary in it, hopping about and chirping. On the front door there was a notice. 'No vacancies. Please do not enquire'. Faded blue shutters hung at the windows.

It was the same house, Abby knew. It gave her that feeling of nervous expectation again. Strange things happened in the Cross. Hadn't Lola said so?

'It was this way,' she said, leading the way,

walking quickly, scanning the street signs. 'I remember the smell of carnations from that stall. Oh, and look! Here's the dress shop. It's even got the same dress in the window. Don't tell me I wouldn't recognize that, Lola, because any woman would.'

Lola came up behind her skeptically.

Abby looked up. The sign that hung above them said 'R. B. Mitchell, Wholesale Toys'. But there was a jeweller's shop next door. She was certain it was the one she had noticed yesterday, although she hadn't observed it as particularly as the black lace frock in the window of the dressmaker's. And surely this was the doorway she had gone in. Although oddly enough the stairs were no longer bare. They now had a rather shabby beige carpet on them.

'But this was the place,' she persisted. 'I'm sure—' Her voice died away uncertainly.

'There you are, Luke,' said Lola. 'An example of the things a woman pinpoints in her memory. Birds in cages, the smell of carnations, a droopy lace dress. These things could be in a dozen streets in the Cross, Abby.'

'What do you think, Abby?' asked Luke. His voice was patient still, but he was obviously agreeing with Lola that she had made some curious mistake.

'I'm going up the stairs,' she said decisively. 'There were two green doors at the top, one to a washroom and one to this other unfurnished room with the man. If they're there I'll know this is the place.'

'Okay, darling,' said Luke, taking her arm.

There was the same curve to the stairs, the same feeling of walking into dimness after the brightness of the street, and of fading noise. And there were two doors at the top, both green.

'There you are,' she said triumphantly. 'Exactly as I said.'

'Even to this notice?' asked Luke.

For the door that yesterday had born no sign at all now had a neat one nailed on it, 'R. B. Mitchell, Toys', and not only that but it was partly open. Luke had only to push it and they were in a small carpeted alcove with a desk, and behind the desk a middle-aged woman, rather fat and jolly looking.

'Good morning,' she said pleasantly. 'Can I help you?'

There was a partition behind her, papered with a striped paper, slightly torn in two places, obviously not new. Neither was the carpet new, nor the worn-looking desk with the ancient model typewriter. Automatically Abby noticed these things. Everything looked as if it had been here for years, including the woman.

On the counter there was a toy, a little wooden figure dressed in starched petticoats, on a swing. Presumably, if it were wound, the figure swung backward and forwards. Abby had the dizzy feeling that it was she on the swing being pushed higher and higher.

'Well, Abby?' said Luke. He spoke to the woman. 'I'm very sorry, but we seem to have come to the wrong place. My wife was looking for a cosmetic company. You don't know it, do you? The Rose Bay Cosmetic Company?'

'Never heard of it. Isn't it more likely to be at Rose Bay?'

Abby's voice had an edge of tension.

'That's exactly what I thought, but it was here I saw it. I came into this room and it was empty. Only yesterday.'

The partition hid the narrow window and the dingy well behind the building. She could scarcely jump over the desk and push her way behind the partition as she had pushed her way in yesterday. This all looked too respectable, and the plump woman wouldn't understand.

'Well, we've been here for twenty-five years. But how much longer we will be, I don't know. Mr. Mitchell is an old man and his toys are old-fashioned. Kids want jeeps and bren guns and rockets nowadays. Not this sort of thing.' She gave the little figure on the swing a push with her stubby finger. Her eyes had an odd brilliance, as if she were excited or keyed up about something. But that was the only off-beat note. The place seemed too genuine for argument.

'You must have been down another street,' she said, looking at Abby. 'You're a stranger here, aren't you? I can tell by your voice.'

'What's behind there?' Abby asked desperately.

'Stock. We're wholesalers. Want to look?'

But Luke was impatient.

'Come, darling. You can't waste people's time. It's obvious you've made a mistake.'

'And I've got to get to work,' said Lola. 'Sorry, hon. I think you've just been having a daydream.'

Abby turned dazedly. She heard Luke saying, 'Thank you very much,' to the woman, and the woman's answer, 'Not at all. Bring your kids for some toys one day. I'll let you have them wholesale.'

Automatically Abby turned to add her thanks. She just caught a flicker of the woman's eyelid. Had she winked at Luke?

Abby clutched his arm as they went down the stairs.

'Is this some unfunny joke? That woman winked at you!'

'Oh, Lord, Abby, don't be so absurd!' Luke's voice was impatient and disbelieving. She knew now that he had never taken her story too seriously. But what did he think she had been doing, inventing a fantasy to get attention? And he, with Lola's help, had had to humor her.

'Luke!' She was near to angry tears. 'I'm sure this was the place. I didn't just make it up. Why should I? Let's ask at the jeweller's.

They'll know in there what's been going on upstairs.'

Lola gave a sigh. 'Honestly, Abby! Anyone can see nothing's gone on upstairs since the year dot. And I've got to fly. Do you mind if I leave you? I'll catch a bus.'

'Thanks a lot, Lola,' said Luke. 'There's no point in staying. If it'll make Abby happier, we'll go into this jeweller's. But I must rush in a moment, too. I'll pick you up tonight, Lola.'

It was better when Lola, with her skeptical eyes, had gone. But Abby was still deeply agitated. She led the way into the small jeweller's shop herself, and when a small gray-haired man peered at her through pince nez over the glass counter she said without preamble,

'Have you ever heard of the Rose Bay Cosmetic Company? Were they upstairs until very recently?'

'The Rose Bay—what kind of company did you say?'

'Cosmetics.'

'Not upstairs, madam. There's a toy company up there.'

Looking into his myopic eyes Abby felt the fog of bewilderment settling over her.

'Then do you know anything about the Rose Bay Company? I'm so sure I saw their sign next door to you yesterday. But now everything looks different. There's even a carpet on the stairs today.'

The man flicked a brief glance to Luke. It looked sympathetic, as if he saw, too, that he must humor Abby's slight mental derangement.

'I never go up there, madam. It isn't part of my premises. But if you say there wasn't carpet yesterday and there is today, you must be confusing it with another place, mustn't you? Things don't happen that quickly with workmen nowadays.'

'Even if it had been put there in the night?' said Abby despairingly.

'Darling, you *have* made a mistake,' Luke said. 'Don't let's go on wasting people's time. My wife insists this company she's looking for was next to a jeweller's,' he explained to the man behind the counter. 'But as I tell her, there isn't only one jeweller's shop in the Cross.'

'But none superior,' said the man, and gave a husky ha ha ha, which put Abby in mind of the kookaburras' satirical laughter. 'Sorry I can't help you, madam.'

'I have this feeling—' Abby began as she and Luke stood in the street.

'*What* feeling?'

'That they're all making fun of me. Deliberately.'

'Me, too?' Luke asked.

Abby looked away unhappily.

'Well, I'm going to ask in this dress shop, anyway. You can't tell me I don't recognize that black lace dress.'

'I might point out that black lace dresses are common enough, or even that you saw this very dress, but at a different time yesterday. Not just as you came down the stairs from the empty room you talk about. You'd had a shock, remember? Or so you say. And you both telephoned Miss Atkinson and had coffee. It was probably after that that you saw the dress.'

'I'm sure—' Again Abby stopped. Was she sure of anything? Perhaps it had been in another street that she had found the dark stairway, beside another dress shop, with another lace dress in its window. Nevertheless she went decisively into the shop.

A very young assistant in a black dress herself, a shabby cotton one, came forward.

'Can I show you something, madam?'

'I just wanted to ask you a question.' The girl had a pallid skin and prominent brown eyes. She was chewing gum, although not ostentatiously. 'Have you ever been upstairs next door?'

The girl looked startled.

'No, I never have. Why?'

'You don't know what office is up there?'

'No. I've only just started working here. I don't know the shops roundabout much. Were you looking for some particular place?'

'The Rose Bay Cosmetic Company,' said Abby clearly.

'That'd be in Rose Bay, wouldn't it? Not up in the Cross.'

Abby shrugged. 'That's what everyone says. But you've never seen their sign in the street?'

'Don't suppose I've looked much.' The girl chewed openly now.

'Can I see your employer?'

'She isn't in yet. She doesn't come in until late morning. She sews at home, you see.'

There was a movement in the doorway and the girl hastily tucked the chewing gum into the corner of her cheek. But it was only a customer, a middle-aged woman, who went to the rack of dresses and began examining them.

' 'Scuse me, madam,' the girl said to Abby. 'I'll have to go.'

'Yes. Thank you very much.'

Luke was waiting outside. He took Abby's arm, and without a word she walked up the street beside him to where he had parked the car. She stopped a minute to stare up at the canary in its cage. A tousled gray head appeared above the massive rubber plant, and stared back, belligerently.

'You looking for vacancies? The sign says none.'

The scrolled iron balcony was very rusty, and shortly must collapse. It was a pity. It was very decorative, much more so than the severe glass and concrete erection next door. It was rather like R. B. Mitchell's toys, reminiscent of another era.

Luke had opened the car door for her.

'I'm not coming yet, Luke. I'm going to stay up here and have some coffee and explore. It's such a fascinating place.'

Luke looked at her. What a contradiction he was. Now his hardness and impatience had gone, and there was that unreadable look in his eyes again. It seemed to be a mixture of tolerance for her stupidity and anxiety lest she imagine herself into any more strange situations.

She would not let Luke's concern affect her, however. She would pursue this mystery by herself.

'But darling, can't you see—'

'I may have made a mistake in the street. I've got to satisfy myself.'

'Then shall I come with you?'

'No, I'd rather be alone.'

He closed the car door and went round to the driver's side.

'All right, then.'

'I don't mean that you didn't help, but you get so impatient, and alone I can take my time. I want to prove to you that I wasn't having an hallucination. Anyway,' she added evenly, 'it's better than going home to have old Jock playing games with me on the telephone.'

'Abby—'

'I'll be all right, Luke. Don't worry about me.' His cool blue eyes looked out at her from the car. 'As you wish. But do be careful.' She had to comfort herself with that last note of urgency in his voice before he drove off.

CHAPTER SEVEN

The canary in its cage began to sing loudly. The old woman who wore a cheap, pink satin kimono leaned over the balcony again to look down at Abby. She had been watering the rubber plant, and her watering can still dripped.

'What's wrong, lass? Had a fight with your boy friend?'

'No. We've been looking for a place we can't find. I don't suppose you've heard of it. The Rose Bay Cosmetic Company.'

'Why don't you look it up in the telephone book?' the woman said practically.

'Of course!' How silly not to think of that. (She had been sure she knew where to find them, but when she had failed why hadn't Luke thought of the telephone book? It was the obvious thing.)

'If you like to wait, I'll look it up for you.'

'Thank you. That is kind of you.'

All the time the woman was away the canary sang deliriously. The sun was growing hotter and even from this distance the scent of carnations from the flower stall was quite distinct. Abby was finding her coat too warm, and wished she had worn a suit. But not the red one. It was too conspicuous. She might have been followed again.

Except that neither Luke nor Lola really believed that had happened. Nor that the Rose Bay Cosmetic Company existed. Because if they had they would have looked up the telephone book.

'Here's the book, ducks,' came the strident voice from the balcony. 'Or what's left of it. You ever kept lodgers? Well, don't, is my advice. They have no respect, I'm telling you. No respect. Wait till I put my specs on. What did you say—Rose Bay? Stone the crows, there's a whole raft of them.'

'Rose Bay Cosmetic Company,' Abby repeated mechanically.

'Ca—ci—co—cob—cow—' The gray head lifted. 'They're not listed, lass.'

'Are you sure?'

'Want to look for yourself?'

'No. Do you think it would be that they've kept their number out of the book?'

'Hardly likely, is it, if they want to do business. What do they sell, face powder, lotions, all that muck?'

'Lipstick,' said Abby.

'Well, goodness, if I was you I'd go into the first chemist and buy yourself another make. No sense quarrelling with your boy friend over a lipstick.'

'No,' Abby agreed desperately.

She remembered to thank the woman. She wondered why she found the juxtaposition of rubber plants and a canary on a crumbling

91

balcony so extraordinarily melancholy. It was just sad to see decay, even picturesque decay. The gray-haired woman in her shabby, pink kimono was part of the ruins.

After an hour's search of all the surrounding streets, peering up every dark stairway and looking twice at every jeweller's shop, she was convinced she hadn't made a mistake. She was also convinced that she must have interrupted the Rose Bay people in the final stages of a move, a flight perhaps (they may have been wanted by too many creditors), and that the toy people had quickly moved in to cover up.

But then why had that cosy and pleasant woman lied? She must have been in the conspiracy. She had had that over-bright and excited look in her eyes. Then was Lola in the conspiracy, too? And Luke? Lola perhaps, for one didn't know what she was up to. And she had shown no surprise at all at finding the toy people in that room.

But surely not Luke! Fiercely Abby rejected that idea, even while remembering that wink, or suspicion of a wink, which the woman had given him.

Miserably she knew there was only one thing to do, and that was to go back up those stairs again, and take another look. Perhaps, alone, the woman would confide in her.

It wasn't easy to make herself do this. Abby hated the moment of leaving the sunshine and entering the cool dark doorway. She could have saved herself the effort, for the green door with its neat sign at the top of the stairs was locked. And this time when she knocked there was no sound from within at all.

She came down the stairs slowly, and went into the dress shop. The same rather vacant-looking girl who obviously didn't remember her came to the counter.

'I wonder if I might borrow your telephone book,' Abby asked.

'Sure.' The girl took the book from beneath the counter and handed it over.

Abby turned to the M's and quickly skimmed the names. It didn't surprise her too much that R. B. Mitchell, Toys, was not listed. There were plenty of Mitchells, even two other R. B.'s, but none in this street, and none called toy sellers. Abby decided that she would have been more surprised to find him in the telephone book than unlisted. She was pretty certain there hadn't been a telephone in that room upstairs yesterday, and quickly as furniture could be shifted, a telephone could not be installed with similar speed.

She wished that she could have seen behind the partition. But it was no use wishing that now, for she couldn't get in.

'The people upstairs go to lunch early,' she observed to the stupid girl.

'Do they? I didn't notice.'

'Is your employer in yet?'

'No, she rang to say she's going to work at home all day today. Say, didn't you come in here before?'

'I did. And you've been very kind.'

'I just don't remember faces,' the girl mumbled. 'Miss Court is always telling me off.'

'What a pity,' said Abby.

It was, too. Because now it was no use asking the girl if she had ever noticed a man with a face like a fish.

*   *   *

When Abby got home in the early afternoon she found a note tucked under the door, 'Flowers left in garage'.

Investigation in the garage revealed a florist's box containing two dozen red carnations. The card said, 'These are to welcome you home—Luke.'

Abby flew up the steps to the front door and unlocked it. Inside, she went straight to the telephone and dialled Luke's number.

'Oh, darling! Your flowers. They're heaven.'

'I'm glad you got them. I'm glad you're home. Have you just come in?'

'Yes. Can't you hear me panting? When I found the flowers I had to rush and ring you.'

'Silly!' But he sounded pleased, and Abby blinked away her tears. 'You see, I can be a thoughtful husband sometimes. I shouldn't have gone off and left you this morning. I was

94

sorry about it, and then I worried about you.'

'But if you didn't believe I was threatened yesterday,' Abby said slowly, 'why should you worry?'

'You're a bit impulsive, my darling. And you look too beautiful to wander about the Cross alone. Tell me, what did happen? You didn't find that mysterious place, did you?'

'No.'

'Then what did you do?' He began to sound impatient again.

'Luke!'

'Yes, darling.'

'Why didn't we think of looking them up in the telephone book?'

'I have. There isn't such a company.'

'But at the beginning, before we left home this morning. Oh, I know I just have a fuzzy mind, but you might have thought of it. Or Lola.'

'Wasn't our object to see the mysterious empty room with the threatening man?'

'I suppose so,' Abby admitted. 'Anyway, for your information, the toys aren't listed either. I believe this is all a cover-up for something else.'

'Abby, please!'

She had put the box of carnations on the table. Their heavy scent was reminding her of the sunny noisy street in the Cross, with the flower stall, and the innocent faces of the shops, and the open doorways leading into dimness. That strange apprehension had come home with her, and was here, in her own house. She wished now that Luke hadn't sent carnations.

'Anyway,' he was saying in his calm sensible way, 'if this were by any wild chance a cover-up for something that you've stumbled on, it's nothing to do with you, and you must just forget it.'

'I'd like to tell the police,' Abby said, and wondered why that thought had just come into her head. 'You never know, this might be a man they're looking for.'

Luke answered quite seriously. 'You'd find it pretty difficult to prove your story. What with the jeweller, and the woman in the toyshop who's obviously been there for years. That was plain enough. Darling, please don't make an ass of yourself.'

Abby took a long breath. She saw that she must put the whole strange disturbing adventure out of her mind. It was only going to have all these unhappy repercussions, arguments with Luke, and Luke almost doubting her sanity. And, as he said, what happened up in Kings Cross was nothing to do with her.

'All right, Luke. Actually, the thing is getting to be a bit of a bore. I'm exhausted, and as you say I've simply wasted my time. Let's not talk of it any more.'

She was rewarded by his relieved tone.

'That's a good girl. Have a rest now. Promise. And I'll be home early.'

So that was that. Abby arranged the carnations in a crystal bowl, and knew that she couldn't put the episode completely out of her mind.

But she could try not to let it obsess her.

A few minutes later the telephone rang. That was when Abby knew most surely that she couldn't forget yesterday's happenings. For now she was absurdly apprehensive about answering the telephone.

She made herself pick it up quickly, and spoke curtly.

A girl's voice with the flat Australian intonation came into her ear.

'Is that Mrs. Fearon?'

'Yes.'

'Miss Moffatt asked me to ring you. She's busy with a client and can't get to the telephone. But she wondered if you could pick up Deirdre from school this afternoon.'

Abby was so relieved that the call was so innocent that she replied willingly,

'Of course I will. But there's nothing wrong, is there?'

'I think her sister has to take her husband to the doctor, or something. She said you'd offered if ever they were stuck.'

'I did. Tell her not to worry. I'll get Deirdre.'

On the whole Abby was pleased to have a

definite errand. In spite of her determination to be sensible, the afternoon might have seemed too long and quiet. Jock's boat was still down there, rocking on the green water, and she didn't want to find herself either watching that hypnotically, or looking up to see if any of the Moffatts were visible.

She would change into a lighter dress and make a cup of tea, then stroll up the road towards Deirdre's school, taking her time. A wind had sprung up, and the scent of the gums would be fragrant and delicious. She would think of Luke's thoughtfulness in sending the flowers, and be happy.

She waved to a dim shape which looked like Mrs. Moffatt behind an upstairs window. But there was no answering wave. For once Mrs. Moffatt must have had her head turned in another direction. It was about three-quarters of a mile to Deirdre's school, up the hill and down the other side, crossing a busy main road where cars flashed by in a constant stream, and then along a quieter street bordered with young gum trees. As Abby approached the school she saw that the children were just coming out. In a few minutes a shouting, screaming, throng had gone by her, some of the children running, some dawdling, some indulging in high-spirited antics. Deirdre would not be among them because she had been told to wait at the gates or in the playground until someone came for her.

The wind was stronger now, tugging at Abby's hair, and whipping her skirt round her legs. The leaves of the gum trees glinted and turned and crackled softly. A group of four nuns was coming down the street, their black garments ballooned into little storm clouds. Abby had to wait for another stream of cars to go by before she could cross the road to the school gates. There was no sign of Deirdre's skinny figure. Expecting to be met by Mary, perhaps she wasn't hurrying. Perhaps she was in one of her states of dawdling boredom.

The playground was reasonably empty of children. Most of them had swept down the street in their eager tide. Abby stood by the gate waiting. The four nuns had stopped at a bus stop and were clustered together, talking earnestly. They seemed to keep turning their heads to look at Abby. Or were they just looking to see if the bus was coming? She wished Deirdre would hurry. Had she been kept in? Being such a lone wolf, she was not likely to stay playing with the other children.

It was almost quiet now, except for the wind in the gum leaves, and the whoosh of passing cars. A dog was tied outside a butcher's shop a little way up the street. It suddenly began to bark frenziedly, then was as abruptly silent. A bus was approaching now. Abby watched to see the four nuns climb on, clutching their heavy skirts. But oddly enough they ignored it, and continued their chatter, and their head-turning towards Abby.

All at once the old prickles of apprehension and suspicion came over her. She was being watched again. But surely not by four holy sisters! Luke would be certain she was suffering from an unnatural obsession if he heard about this.

She had to act. She couldn't just stand there having foolish fears. She turned abruptly and went into the school grounds. To the first child within hearing, a stout freckled little boy, she said, 'Have you seen Deirdre Moffatt? Do you know if she's been kept in?'

'Deirdre Moffatt? Don't know her, Miss. Oh, you mean Deirdre!'

'A thin little girl. Straight hair.'

'Yes, I know her, Miss. Her name's Deirdre Henderson.'

Of course—Deirdre did have a father whose name she bore. One just never thought of her as anything but a Moffatt.

'She isn't here today, Miss. She must be sick.'

'Are you sure?' Abby exclaimed.

Her intensity made the little boy suddenly shy and awkward.

'She's in my class, and she wasn't there.'

A football bounced near, and, glad to escape from a stranger, the boy leaped after it, shouting.

Abby hurried back to the street. Her mouth was dry, her heart beating too fast. Who was the woman who had telephoned her? Was she genuinely someone who worked with Lola? Or was she an accomplice of the fish-faced man—the man who had said sniggeringly, 'Is that the little lady in red?'

She had to wait to cross the street again. The cars swept down at high speed. Everything was whirling at her. All the faces behind the steering wheels seemed friendly, but in too much of a hurry. They had no time to realize her more urgent hurry. Another bus was coming up to the stop, and this time, in a little flurry of activity, the nuns climbed aboard and were carried off.

Abby was quite alone in the glittering afternoon. And very frightened.

Reaching the top of the street at last, she could see the wide blue harbor and the great arch of the bridge. Nearer, she could look down to the green river, the faded gray roof of the Moffatts' house, and the scarlet of the poinsettias in her own garden. She had to slow her pace a little to get her breath after hurrying so much up the slope. There were not many people about here, some children playing with a dog, and at the end of the street a little tableau, the stooping figure of Mary pushing Milton in his wheel chair.

They were just about to turn the corner. Forgetting her weariness, Abby began to run. Before Mary was within hearing she had turned the corner. She seemed to be hurrying, too. Probably Milton was ill-temperedly saying he didn't like being stared at. Or else that he was tired from his visit to the doctor.

Abby ran all the way down the street, but by the time she, too, had turned the corner, Mary was just disappearing through the gate to the big house. She seemed to hesitate for a moment, and turned her head. Abby waved wildly and called. But Mary didn't hear, and went on in.

It was Mrs. Moffatt who answered the door a few minutes later in response to Abby's frantic ringing.

'Why, Abby!' she said in surprise and pleasure. 'You look so hot. Have you been hurrying?'

'Yes, I was trying to catch up with Mary and Milton.'

'They've just come in. Milton had to go to the doctor today instead of tomorrow, as usual.' The old lady peered closer with her wrinkled lizard's eyes. 'Has something upset you?'

'Is Deirdre home?' Abby asked.

'Yes, she's been home all day. She got sick, or she said she felt sick, just after you all left this morning. I'm not sure it wasn't an excuse to stay home from school, but I said that if she stayed home she had to stay in bed. See which she liked best, school or bed. So she's in her room now. Did you want to see her?'

Abby leaned against the door. She felt

foolishly breathless and weak.

'Then can you explain why I got a telephone message to meet her at school?'

'To meet Deirdre? Today? You mean, Lola rang you?'

'No, it wasn't Lola. It was someone who worked with her. Or so she said. Mary had to take Milton to the doctor, so could I possibly collect Deirdre.'

Mrs. Moffatt said, 'Good gracious! But Lola knew Deirdre was sick. Mary rang her.'

At that moment Mary appeared in the hall. She didn't look as if she had been hurrying, for her face was quite pale. Although when she came nearer Abby could see the faint shine of perspiration.

'What are you saying, mother? Who did I ring?'

'Abby says she had a message to get Deirdre from school, but I'm just telling her you rang Lola to say the child was sick. So who could possibly have rung Abby?'

Mary's eyes widened. 'How odd! And you went all the way for nothing, Abby?'

'It was someone who knew you were taking Milton to the doctor,' Mrs. Moffatt added.

'That's not so strange. I left over an hour ago. Anyone watching would see that.'

'But who?' said Abby.

'Yes, who?' repeated Mrs. Moffatt. 'And why?'

Abby had to admit the basis for her fear at

last.

'I expect it was to get me out of the house.'

Mary gave a gasp, and Mrs. Moffatt's hand went to her throat. But in a moment the old lady had recovered herself and declared indignantly, 'Now wouldn't that be the meanest thing, to get you out of the house by a trick like that. Are you afraid to go home? I'll come with you. I'm not afraid of burglars.'

The faint purr of wheels on polished floor sounded, and there was Milton looking extraordinarily fit, as if the outing had done him good.

'Has someone had a burglary? Abby, surely nothing's happened in your house.'

'We don't know yet,' said Mrs. Moffatt briskly. 'But someone has used a mean excuse to get Abby out of the house for half an hour. And moreover when you also were out, Milton, because otherwise you'd have been at the window, wouldn't you? You might have seen something. I've just been taking a nap, and Deirdre has, too.'

'Abby, shall I come down?' Milton asked. For the first time Abby saw his handsome face without its look of frustration and anger. He looked alert and interested. One could not have said there was any sympathy in his expression, but as yet there was no proof that sympathy was needed.

'Darling, you can't manage that slope,' Mary fluttered anxiously. 'And you know I can't hold your chair on it.'

'Damn, damn, damn!' Milton exclaimed, his moment of kindness gone. He thumped uselessly on the arms of the chair.

'Don't, Milton!' whispered Mary. 'Mother's going, anyway.

'I'm not afraid to go alone,' said Abby. 'I was only asking about Deirdre. Her safety's more important than Luke's and my few things.'

She felt almost calm now, and only wanted to get to the bottom of the mystery. Perhaps nothing had happened at all. Everything seemed to melt foggily into this kind of limbo, and the things which, for some perfectly good reason, she had done became quite meaningless.

'I'm coming with you,' said Mrs. Moffatt, flapping after her in her bedroom slippers.

A lizard flashed out of Abby's path, an elongated shadow, swift as sound. She noticed that the house looked exactly as she had left it, closed, with the curtains drawn. Jock's boat rocked gently on the green glass water. One of the kookaburras flew out of the jacaranda tree and perched, a cosy shape, feathers fluffed, on the chimney. Even when she had put her key into the keyhole and opened the door there was nothing different, no sound.

Breathing heavily behind her, Mrs. Moffatt whispered, 'Is it all right?'

All at once Abby was glad to have her there,

for she knew that it wasn't all right. The bowl of carnations which she had put on the hall table were ever so slightly disarranged, as if someone had brushed past them quickly. One of the blooms was hanging almost out of the water.

Abby stood still, motioning Mrs. Moffatt to do the same. The old lady's breathing was very audible. 'What is it, dear?' she whispered tensely.

There was no sound in the house. No one was there now. A curtain billowed out in the kitchen where a window stood wide open. Abby was almost certain she hadn't left it open.

'Someone's been and gone,' she said, as if speaking to herself. 'Like that lizard I just saw.'

But the only room in a state of chaos was the bedroom. There drawers were turned upside down and things flung about.

'Lordy!' said Mrs. Moffatt. 'Your jewellery! That's what he was after. Did you have much?'

'No. Very little. He wouldn't have got much out of that.'

She was wearing her only treasured piece, Luke's diamond engagement ring.

'I'll have to ring the police,' she said dazedly.

It didn't matter much what had gone, it really didn't matter at all in comparison with the fact that hers and Luke's bedroom was smirched and desecrated.

'Dear, dear, dear!' said Mrs. Moffatt. 'And to think the thief used Deirdre as his weapon. Little innocent Deirdre!'

'Professional burglars always study their victims' habits,' Abby said mechanically. 'I expect I've been watched for some time.' Automatically her gaze went down to Jock's boat. Jock had a very good idea of the pattern of her days. He had even had the impertinence to call at her back door. Had refusing him work caused him to have his revenge? But how foolish that would be, unless he planned to leave the river at once, before the police came.

'I'm going to ring Luke first,' Abby said.

'How can you be so calm? All your pretty things scattered about like this.' The old lady picked up a pale blue nightdress and her face looked more lizard-like than ever in its lugubrious bewilderment.

'I'm not calm at all,' said Abby. She felt a little sick, and, for some reason, much more frightened than the occasion seemed to deserve. It was this happening so easily in broad daylight that made it worse, as if the burglar were having a macabre joke.

When she got on to Luke he said in a controlled voice, 'Good God! I'll come home right away. Don't do anything till I get there. Are you alone?'

'Mrs. Moffatt's here.'

'Good. Then you girls sit down and have a cup of tea. Don't touch anything in the bedroom.'

He hung up without even thinking to ask her what had been stolen. Which was as well, because so far she hadn't found anything at all missing, not even her one good string of pearls.

Luke arrived in a short enough time to suggest that he had exceeded speed limits all the way. He looked briefly at the devastation in the bedroom, and went straight to the telephone to ring the police. His face was furious.

The burglar had found the catch on the kitchen window easy enough to open. There was only a little denting in the woodwork, and no broken glass.

'We'll have to get better locks,' Luke said.

'This is Australia, not South Kensington,' Abby said nervously. 'I didn't think burglaries were so frequent.'

'They come in waves,' said Mrs. Moffatt. 'I've known as many as six people being done in a week, then nothing for months. The burglars have moved to another area. I hope this isn't a sign that this part is becoming fashionable again. Though goodness knows we haven't much to lose. I sold all my jewellery long ago.' The little wrinkled face smiled up at Abby in its anxious, friendly way. 'Don't be too upset, dear. Now you've your husband to look after you I'll go. And I hope you won't still find that something valuable is missing.'

*   *   *

'Nothing missing, you say,' said the young policeman fingering his notebook.

'My wife says not, as far as she can discover.'

'He must have been disturbed, then. Perhaps you got back too quick, Mrs. Fearon. Could you identify this voice on the telephone again?'

'I don't think so. All Australian voices sound alike to me. But it was someone who knew our names and our habits.'

'Easy enough to find that out. That's an old trick of burglars. We'll do some tests for fingerprints, but it looks to me this man's too professional. He won't have left any prints. It's my guess he came by water.'

'Up the river!' Involuntarily Abby looked out at Jock's shabby boat, lying low in the water.

'Yeah. He wouldn't run the risk of being overlooked by anyone in the house up there, then. He could leave his boat down there and slip up the rocks. Who's is that boat anchored over there?'

'Oh, that's old Jock's,' Luke explained. 'He's an odd job man who lives down there and does a few jobs ashore.'

'Then I'll have a word with him.'

The two men went out to hail the boat. But there was no answer. No lanky figure appeared on the deck. The boat looked deserted.

It wouldn't be, though. Abby was convinced old Jock was aboard and lying low. He would know what had been going on. She was sure he would.

However, before the police left half an hour later, Jock had appeared, slouching down the road, a knapsack slung on his shoulder. He made to scramble down the short cut to the river's edge.

When he saw the police car he stopped and stared. There was nothing furtive about his actions. He was obviously astonished and inquisitive.

One of the police, the younger man, went over and questioned him. He gesticulated a lot and once gave a high whinnying laugh.

The man came back, shaking his head.

'He looks a natural, doesn't he? But he's got an alibi. He's been doing a gardening job for Mrs. Brookman of Silver Street. Got there at noon, and has just stopped work. Mrs. Brookman was there all the time, he says. She made him tea at three o'clock. That's approximately the time this job was done here. So it looks as if your swagman is in the clear.'

'So he's not even a witness,' said Luke thoughtfully.

'Well, we'll get going,' said the policeman. 'We'll let you know if we get on to anything. But these fellows—they're like lizards. Vanish without a trace, and just as quickly. I'd advise you to get some double locks.'

*   *   *

As soon as they were alone Luke turned to Abby.

'Put on your prettiest dress. We're going out to dinner.'

Abby looked at him uncertainly.

'Do you think we should leave the house?'

'The damned house can take care of itself.'

Abby's resilient spirits began to rise.

'What fun! Where shall we go? What shall I wear? Isn't it lucky my pearls weren't stolen? I wonder what that burglar thought he would find. Perhaps he expected me to have brought heirlooms from England. I'll have time for a bath, won't I?'

If Luke had stopped to think he might have realized that it was very rarely in the eight weeks she had been here that Abby had felt like behaving in her normal high-spirited way. But fury still smouldered in his eyes and he was thinking of something else.

'Take as much time as you like. It's early yet. I've got some people to telephone.'

From the bedroom Abby heard him talking to Miss Atkinson, giving her detailed instructions about some work. She went to run a bath, and as the water roared from the taps happily dawdled over manicuring her nails, undressing and scenting the water. Let's live only in the present moment, she kept telling herself. Tonight there would be no melancholy sunset, for Luke was here and they were going to have a party. For once he had been jolted out of his preoccupation with work and other things, and put her first.

She turned the tap off, and in the sudden silence heard Luke's voice.

'You complete and utter fool! Of all the melodramatic and unnecessary things . . . What? . . . Not trust me! . . . I'm sorry, too . . .'

Then he must have realized the silence in the house, for abruptly he lowered his voice and the rest of his sentence was inaudible.

He was probably still talking to Miss Atkinson, and one wondered how her middle-aged aplomb would react to that telling off. Or had he taken the opportunity, under cover of the roaring bath water, to ring someone else.

Abby refused to let suspicions spoil her happiness.

'Luke, surely you're not talking to Miss Atkinson like that! I'd never have the courage.'

'She's made a stupid mistake.'

'Miss Atkinson! I'm sure she never makes mistakes.' She was still speaking lightly, hiding her disquiet. 'Who is it who doesn't trust you?'

'A client. An important one. How long are you going to be?'

'Hours.' She pushed away the thought of the distrustful client. 'I'm going to make every minute of this evening last.'

'Have you hated it all so much?' came his unexpected question.

So he had noticed, after all. He hadn't been too preoccupied for that.

Abby tried to speak casually. 'Darling, open the door if we're going to talk. Have I hated what?'

'Being here alone.'

'Well—a little. As it grew dark at nights. Have you noticed how the cypresses and the monastery on the hill stand out against the sunset? They didn't make me feel religious, just depressed.'

'Would you like to live somewhere else?' Again his question was unexpected, and startled her.

'Leave here?'

'I thought after the things that had happened you might want to. If you do, we will.'

Abby thought longingly of a house on the other side of the city, away from the river, away from the watching Moffatts. She scrambled out of the bath and wrapping herself in a towel opened the door.

'Do you really mean that—' She saw that he was feeling the wood of the door thoughtfully, and suddenly she realized his pride in the house he had planned and built. She also realized how fatal a mistake it would be to insist on moving.

'Luke, how absurd can you get? You built

113

this house for me and I love it. Nothing would make me move.'

Her lie must have been convincing, for he took her damp, flushed face in his hands. His own above hers was searching, desperately serious.

'I would if you were unhappy.'

When she shook her head he seemed to relax.

'Bless you,' he said.

And that brief moment made it all worth while, the loneliness and the strange fears, Jock's persistent pop songs, the unexplained telephone calls, and the wreckage in the bedroom this afternoon. Even whomever it was Luke had just called a fool. Because she knew it couldn't have been Miss Atkinson.

It was while she waited in the living-room for Luke to finish dressing that her uneasiness, like a recurring disease, increased. She hadn't drawn the curtains and in the dim light she thought she saw two figures on Jock's boat. She couldn't be sure. Jock was on the deck, but it seemed as if a shadow had moved across the cabin porthole.

The police had suggested that the burglar might have come by the river. Supposing he had been on Jock's boat all the time! Then it didn't matter that Jock did have an alibi. Indeed, it could have been he who had rung Abby with the fictitious message while his confederate waited to see her leave the house.

The fish-faced man, she thought, with her usual method of jumping to fantastic conclusions.

Fantastic or not, the conviction would not leave her.

'Luke,' she called urgently. 'I think Jock's got a friend on his boat.'

'Well, what of it?' Luke had come to the door. 'Darling, help me with my tie.'

'But I've got this funny feeling it's the fish-faced man. You know the one—'

'I know the one.' Luke maintained his pleasant tolerant expression. 'You can see in the dark, I imagine.'

'No, I can't see his face. I just feel it's him. If it is, he was the burglar.'

'All right,' said Luke, tugging at his tie, 'we'll go over and see.'

'Now?' Abby squeaked. Suddenly the river looked very dark and cold. She could almost feel its chill on her skin.

'Don't tell me I don't humor your fancies. You may even be right for once.'

'Luke, you're laughing at me again,' Abby pleaded.

'On the contrary, I've never laughed at you. Far from it. Come on, let's go. Don't look so worried. I used to row for my school. I won't splash your dress or tip you into the river. But what I won't stand is you sitting here indulging in fancies.'

Abby made a last nervous protest.

115

'We can't go on the river in evening dress.'

'Why not? Jock will be flattered.'

Abby found herself bustled out of the house into the windy twilight. At least one thing her husband liked was action. Perhaps he was right. Perhaps that was one reason she loved him.

He helped her down the narrow rocky path to the water's edge. Jock's lanky figure had disappeared into the lighted cabin.

'Aren't you even going to call out and tell him we're coming?' Abby asked.

'And then have you say his friend had time to slip overboard?'

'Luke, you are laughing at me. Besides, he'll hear us coming, anyway.'

But Jock had his favorite record playing and clearly hadn't heard the splash of oars. For when the dinghy grated alongside he appeared in some surprise. He had only his shabby denim trousers on, and was hugging his naked chest against the chilly wind.

'Hullo, mate. Want something?'

'Just taking my wife for a row. She's curious about your boat. She wonders how anyone can live comfortably in so small a space.'

'You can do that all right,' said Jock, grinning and showing his stained stumps of teeth. 'Want to come aboard and look? I got everything but a washing machine. Honest.'

He pulled the canvas curtain back from the lighted cabin. A strong smell of cooking fish came out.

The record was running down. '*I love only you-oo . . .*' Jock bent to switch it off. He grinned invitingly.

'Coming aboard, Mrs. Fearon? You look dressed for a party. Afraid I've only got beer.'

'Thank you, but we were just—having some fresh air.'

The excuse was lamentable. This man could read right into her mind. He knew her suspicions and was enjoying them.

'Catch that burglar?' he asked insolently.

'Not yet,' said Luke. 'We will.'

'Fair enough, mate. Too much of that sort of thing going on. Sorry if the music disturbs you, Mrs. Fearon. I have it on a lot, being alone all the time.'

His glinting eyes held Abby's. Luke said easily,

'Well, darling? Getting cold? We'd better go. We'll call again one day.'

Jock nodded cheerfully.

'You do that, mate. Glad to see you any time.'

Neither of them spoke until they got ashore. Then Luke made a deplorable joke.

'If your friend was on board you don't need to worry any more. He was being cooked for supper.' He took her rigid arm. 'Joke, sweetie, joke. There was no one else there, as you could see.'

A large winged creature, black in the dusk,

117

flew in Abby's face. She gave a small scream and had to cling to Luke, forgiving him for his facetiousness. Australia! she was thinking. Where things flew out of the dark into your face, where everyone called you 'mate' and burgled your house when your back was turned, where your husband became a stranger . . .

'I promise not to imagine things again,' she said in a small voice. 'Can we still have fun tonight?'

'If you'll take that suspicious look out of your eyes. Everything's all right, darling. I promise you it is.'

He spoke with such conviction that Abby had the fleeting thought that he must have secretly solved the whole mystery, including the identity of the burglar. Or that he had known everything that was going on all the time . . .

There was one more small tableau involving the Moffatt family that evening.

As Luke drove the car slowly up past the big house Abby caught a glimpse of Deirdre in the lighted window of her room. She had her back to the night, and was holding out the skirts of an obviously new dress to show somebody. For the first time since Abby had known her she looked like a normal little girl, excited about a new dress.

Was there any significance in Lola remembering to buy it for her today, the day

she had to stay in her room whether her illness
was genuine or pretended?

CHAPTER EIGHT

Lola was over early the next morning. She had come to say she was sorry about the burglary and had anything developed?

'I came over last night but there was no one home. I am sorry about this, Abby, especially since I was brought into it. Fancy using Deirdre as a decoy! I was hopping mad about that. Now you'll never trust me if I do take you up on that offer of yours.'

'Of course I'll trust you,' said Abby, knowing she never would. 'How is Deirdre today?'

'A bit peaky. She's staying home from school. It's her birthday, anyway, and thank goodness I remembered to buy her her new dress. I believe she's going to ask you to a party. You ought to be flattered. It's the first time she's ever wanted to ask anyone.'

'She should have other children,' Abby protested.

Lola shrugged. 'Deirdre's Deirdre. I believe she was born old.'

But at least this explained the reason for Lola at last remembering to buy the dress. There was nothing suspicious about it being last night, after a day when Deirdre had kept so carefully out of sight.

She watched Luke and Lola drive off. Luke

had said she was to ring the office and talk to Miss Atkinson, at least, if he wasn't in, if anything at all worried her. Now that something that was not just one of her peculiar fancies had happened, he was prepared to be sympathetic and remorseful about her distress. He had proved that by offering to find another house if she wanted to move from here. She was glad she had refused to do that. He would inevitably despise her a little if she ran away. It was certain that he had not wanted to move.

But she hoped, all the same, that she didn't have to watch him and Lola drive off every morning like this. Lola's head was turned to Luke's, and they were already deep in conversation.

Deirdre came over as Abby was feeding the kookaburras. They immediately swooped off to the jacaranda tree, clacking their beaks in rage. Deirdre stood quite still staring at them. Abby wondered whose stare was the more malevolent, the birds' or the child's.

'Hullo, Deirdre. Happy birthday. Why didn't you tell me you were having a birthday?'

Deirdre ignored the question and asked the one of her own which she had obviously come to ask.

'What did the burglar take?'

'Nothing, so far as we can discover.'

'Then why did he come?'

'I suppose he thought I had more jewellery than I have. Do I look to you like someone who has tiaras and things?'

'Were you scared?'

'Yes, I was. Were you really sick?'

Deirdre blinked again and scuffed her feet.

'I felt sick. Gran said I looked pale. Anyway, I hate school.'

'But you didn't know the burglar was going to ring me up?'

'No, no, no!'

Abby didn't know why she had asked that question, but neither did she expect such a violent denial, as if Deirdre, poor little scrap, had been worrying about her innocent part in the plot. She was alarmingly perceptive.

Or else she had guiltily contributed her part to the plot . . .

'I saw you in your new dress last night. You were standing at the window. It looked very chic.'

'What does that mean?'

'Oh, it means rather specially fashionable.'

'Good God, I don't want to be fashionable!' said Deirdre. 'Why don't you get the kookies back?'

'They won't come while you're here.'

'Don't they like me either?'

'You silly little creature. Who else do you imagine doesn't like you?'

'Uncle Milton,' said the child flatly. 'He says I'll have to go to boarding school. I poke about too much. It's only because I found his chair yesterday. I thought he was in it, but he wasn't.

There was only a lot of pillows and a rug. It looked just like a man, anyway. I pushed it down the hall.' She flashed round at Abby. 'Well, I couldn't help it if he was in the toilet.' She began to giggle. 'And then, you see, he couldn't get out because I'd wheeled the chair away. He was yelling for Mary. He can only walk two steps on his sticks. So now,' she finished, 'they say I have to go to boarding school. If you ask me, all this persecution started because I took that lipstick of Mummy's.'

'Persecution! What words you use.'

'It's what they do to martyrs,' Deirdre explained, looking martyred. 'Are you using the lipstick?'

'Of course.'

'Oh, good. I'm glad the burglar didn't take it.'

'That's not a thing burglars usually take,' Abby said mildly.

'I don't know. It had a gold case. They'd look for gold, wouldn't they? Will you wear the lipstick to my party tonight?'

'Am I being invited to your party?'

'If you want to come,' said Deirdre indifferently.

'Who else will be there?'

'Oh, just us. My father might come.'

'Your fa—' Abby swung the child round. 'Deirdre, what is this? You didn't tell me your father was home.'

'He isn't home, but he's in Sydney. Mummy was talking to someone on the telephone. She said "Now Reg is back—"' The narrow pale eyes looked up at Abby. 'Reg is his name.'

'But why don't you ask your mother?' Abby said. 'Surely she'd tell you.'

'What's the use? No one tells me anything. They say I'm not to be trusted.' Deirdre picked up a stone and threw it at the kookaburras, making them fly off. 'Neither am I.' She giggled suddenly. 'Uncle Milton was furious. Absolutely furious.'

'What about?'

'About being stuck in the toilet, of course. But honestly there were so many pillows there was no room for him in that old chair.'

Suddenly the kookaburras, sitting safely in the gum tree at the end of the garden, began to laugh raucously. Haw, haw, haw, ho, ho ho . . .

'Deirdre,' said Abby urgently, 'does someone still walk in your house at night?'

'Sometimes. I don't always hear because I'm asleep. Now I'm not sure if it's old Jock or my father. I think it's father.' She looked up with her sly glance. 'But you don't have to believe me. I tell lies, they say.'

'Are you telling me lies now?'

There was a rapping at the big window of the Moffatts' house. Mary's face shone palely.

'Deirdre! Deirdre, come in out of the sun. You know you've been sick.'

124

'Deirdre! Are you telling lies when you say you think your father walks in the house at night?'

For answer Deirdre gave a clever imitation of the kookaburras' sardonic laughter.

'See you tonight at my party,' she shouted, running off. Her narrow, foxy little face was mocking and defiant. Under the defiance Abby sensed the fear. With cold certainty she knew the child was hiding some nightmare . . .

And that brought her back herself into the dreary circle of confusion and apprehension and doubt. Doubt of everyone, including her own husband . . .

*   *   *

Again the sun shone in the brazen sky. Before it got too hot, Abby went into the garden to plant out the box of geraniums that had arrived yesterday. She planned a border along the house where the ground had already been prepared. Even so, it was a hot, tiring task. Lizards flashed out of sight, and a spider much too large for comfort scuttled under a rock. The geraniums already showed tips of color, brilliant crimsons and scarlets. Pastel colors were wrong in this country. Everything had to be vivid and flaring, even the red earth.

Abby was aware of Jock watching her from his boat, probably resentful that yesterday she had refused him work, and now did a hot, tedious task herself. The eyes would be at the Moffatts' windows, too. Why had she been so foolish as to refuse Luke's offer to move? Why had she let Luke's fondness for a place he had planned and built sway her? She shouldn't be so impulsive and self-sacrificing. Because in the end this place would get her down. She knew it would. She couldn't be treated like a goldfish in a pool forever, watched and poked at and talked about. It would have been wiser to uproot Luke at the beginning.

She had been swayed by a moment of sentiment, not wanting to bring more of that strange anxiety to Luke's face.

For even he must have known that burglary had something phoney about it. Lola's protestations of innocence, Jock's convenient alibi, Mrs. Moffatt's anxious care of her that did not include alarm. Surprisingly did not include alarm . . . Deirdre's new dress, remembered at last . . . Round and round the thoughts went in Abby's brain, as intolerable as the flies that buzzed about her hot face.

Were they all just trying to frighten her? For some reason of their own? Perhaps to drive her away so that Lola could have Luke, because she had always regarded him as her property . . .

Even Deirdre's present of the lipstick might have been engineered, anticipating what Luke's reaction would be . . .

'Abby! Abby!'

Abby started up, straightening her aching back. Mary was coming down the path.

'You look so hot down there. Mother said to bring you up for a cold drink. You shouldn't work in the sun like that. You'll soon learn not to.'

Mary looked cool in her green cotton dress. But she always looked cool. If anything upset her she only went more pale and quiet. It was a pity, Abby thought, that she had this inward shrinking from all the Moffatts, for Mary looked as if she needed a friend.

There was nothing to do now but to accept the invitation.

'Thank you, Mary, I'd love a cold drink. Just let me wash.'

The shutters were half closed in the Moffatts' drawing-room, and the dim light was faintly green. They were all there, Mrs. Moffatt, Mary, Milton and Deirdre. A tray with tall glasses and a jug of iced beer stood on the table.

Mrs. Moffatt put aside her piece of tapestry and wools to welcome Abby. She had more beads than ever round her scrawny neck, and looked like a colored chandelier. Her little, brown face smiled eagerly.

'Abby dear, have you recovered from that nasty upset yesterday? Lola says the police discovered nothing, not even fingerprints. Burglars are too clever nowadays. I once saw a picture of a burglar's kit. There were amazing things in it, even to some sort of article that looked like knitting needles.'

'I believe they now use a kind of periscope to put through the keyhole,' Milton observed. 'Mary, are you getting us drinks?'

Mary sprang up to fill the tall glasses. Ice chinked with a cool sound.

'It's really extraordinarily hot for early spring. We'll still get plenty of cold nights. Will you have some beer, Abby?'

'What are you planting in the garden, Abby?' Mrs. Moffatt asked.

'Geraniums.'

'Very nice. Naturally we're interested, since you comprise our view. We must get something done about our garden, Mary.'

'I know, Mother. When I get time. Wouldn't it be nice to be rich, and employ someone else to do all the work.'

'But can't we afford someone? Even one man?'

Milton looked at Abby.

'This is our favorite conversation; dreaming of being rich. One never knows, miracles can happen. My wife believes so, anyway.'

Mary smiled, but there was something unreadable in her dark eyes. She did have some dream, of course. It would be an escapist one, in which, first of all, her husband could walk again. Poor Mary. Dreaming didn't accomplish anything except making the present endurable.

'Well, did you have a nice time last night?' Mrs. Moffatt asked briskly, changing the subject.

'Wonderful, thank you,' Abby answered, and thought that like Deirdre she was telling lies. For the evening hadn't been a success. Much as he had struggled to be attentive and entertaining, Luke had not been able to keep up his pretence of gaiety. There had been long silences between them, and that odd constraint that was now almost always there. There had been candlelight and music and good food. And they had made conversation like two rather nervous strangers who had just met.

Yet this morning Luke had driven away with Lola talking animatedly.

'Wasn't Luke thoughtful, to whisk you away like that from your unpleasant experience. It was just what you needed.'

'Yes,' said Abby and turned to Milton. 'I hope you got a good report from the doctor yesterday.'

'Oh, the usual. The usual.' Milton's dark brows frowned. He moved his large, strong hands restlessly on the arms of the chair. 'He had the nerve to suggest occupational therapy. I told him I was interested in nothing but walking. If one of his charming therapists could teach me that, I'd listen.'

Mary touched his shoulder.

'You will, Milton. You will.'

She must drive him mad with her hovering,

Abby thought. Yet what else was there for it, unless he went to some kind of institution.

'Milton goes into hospital again next Monday,' she explained to Abby. 'He always gets keyed up before that. But perhaps it won't be so painful this time, love.'

'I could stand the pain if it accomplished something. Well, for heaven's sake, don't let's sit here talking about a hulk like me. You know I can't stand it.'

He glowered again at his wife, and she smiled placatingly.

'Of course not. Does Abby know we're planning a week-end away first? We're going kangaroo shooting. Milton enjoys that. Don't you, darling?'

'Make the blighters jump,' Milton muttered.

'And you're to stay with me,' Mrs. Moffatt said to Abby. 'Naturally you don't want to do anything so bloodthirsty. Lola said you didn't care for the idea at all.'

'No, I don't. I think it's gruesome.'

Milton looked at her with his pale, prominent eyes. He didn't bother to hide his contempt.

'Then you'd better stay here. We'll only be away a couple of days. Luke enjoys it.'

'Has he been before?' Abby asked, thinking that here was something else Luke hadn't told her.

'Not with us. But every good Australian knows how to use a gun. Lola's as useful as a

130

man with one. Not Mary, though. She's squeamish. Aren't you, my love?'

Mary flinched from his contempt. Abby realized she hated the thought of the expedition, but that she had to go because of Milton. No one else could look after him. He wanted her around. She wouldn't dare to oppose him.

Who would, thought Abby, looking at his strong introspective face. His illness made him mean, but did he need to be that mean? She decided to throw a stone into the cool murky pool of this drawing-room.

'Deirdre says she's having a birthday party tonight, and wants me to come.'

'That's right, dear. You can, can't you?' Mrs. Moffatt was smiling eagerly.

'Yes. I'd love to. Especially to meet Deirdre's father.'

The stone crashed almost audibly. There was a shattered silence. Then Mrs. Moffatt said bewilderedly,

'What has Deirdre been telling you? That her father has come home? But she isn't always truthful, I'm afraid.'

She looked towards the child who sat in a corner, her head bent over a book. Her hair was hanging over her eyes. She had no intention of being lured into looking up and meeting anybody's reproachful gaze.

'Good gracious!' said Mary. 'What else has she been telling you, Abby? I saw her having a long conversation with you this morning.'

'She told us that Barry Smith had broken all those pieces of her jigsaw puzzle,' said Mrs. Moffatt. 'When she knows very well Barry hasn't been here for months. She won't have him to play. I'm afraid she did the damage herself, quite deliberately.'

'She'll have to be sent to boarding school,' Milton said impatiently. 'I keep on telling you. She's growing into a barbarian. And an untruthful one at that.'

'It's her birthday,' Abby said involuntarily.

'All the more reason why she shouldn't tell lies,' declared Mrs. Moffatt. 'Really, Deirdre. How can you be so wicked?'

Deirdre lifted a haughty face.

'I happen to know my father might come tonight. I just happen to know.'

'And how do you happen to know?' asked her grandmother.

'No one here tells me anything. So why should I tell people things?'

'You see?' said Mrs. Moffatt helplessly.

Milton added in a grimly satisfied voice, 'I've been telling you this for long enough. The child's impossible. She even steals things, as you know. She took that lipstick of her mother's and gave it away. That's the true sign of a disturbed mentality.'

And whose fault was it that she had a disturbed mentality, Abby thought furiously. Whose fault? Her casual butterfly mother's, or these other two women revolving timidly round a sick man? Or the missing father's?

She put down her glass, saying quietly and pointedly, 'I don't suppose she was born with a disturbed mentality. I hardly think any child is. And now I must go. Thank you for the drink. I'll be seeing you tonight. I hope you have a cake with candles, Deirdre.'

'That baby stuff!' said Deirdre, with her usual vigor. She had developed armor, that little one. Angry words slid off her fragile shoulders.

'Well, at least I hope you wear your new dress.'

Abby smiled again politely, and made her thankful departure. What a family! How could Luke stand them? Except that poor little wretch, Deirdre, of course. The child who seemed to have no attractive attributes except her name.

Abby decided to go shopping this afternoon to find her a birthday present, something that would appeal even to her unorthodox and unchildish taste.

CHAPTER NINE

Abby knew she was going up to Kings Cross again. She had promised Luke to forget the foolish mix-up and he trusted her promise. But since then her suspicions had been aroused again, chiefly because the Moffatt family couldn't let her forget that lipstick. She felt certain that it was the clue to the whole mystery, and if Luke couldn't, or wouldn't, explain it, she would find out for herself.

She had begun by going into one of the large George Street stores and asking the buyer behind the cosmetics counter if she ever bought the products of the Rose Bay Cosmetic Company.

'I've never heard of them,' the woman answered. 'Where are they? In Rose Bay?'

Or in liquidation, Abby thought.

'I don't know. I'm trying to trace them myself. They make a particular lipstick that I like.'

'Oh? What is it called?'

'Galah.'

'Well, I never. After the parrots, I suppose. Clever. But it's never been advertised, as far as I know. If it had done well I'd have heard of it. We just deal with the well-known names here, Arden, Rubenstein and so on. We've a nice new range of colors if you'd like to see them.'

'Sorry,' said Abby. 'I really did want this one.'

'I don't think you'll find any of the big stores stock it. I'll make some enquiries if you like. If you leave your telephone number I'll ring you if I find out anything.'

'That's very kind of you.'

'Not at all. You've got me interested now. Galah. That's an intriguing name. Sure you don't want anything else? Skin lotion, perfume?'

'All I'm shopping for today is a birthday present for an eight year old.'

'Oh well, then, you'd want a toy of some kind, wouldn't you? Books and toys are on the fourth floor.'

'A toy,' Abby repeated slowly, and that was when she decided to go back to Kings Cross. For now she had the perfect reason to go up those stairs again, and to get behind that partition to see R. B. Mitchell's stock of toys. If any . . .

*　　　*　　　*

The door still bore the inscription 'R. B. Mitchell, Toys', but it was shut, as somehow Abby had expected it to be. She also knew that there was no use in knocking. Nobody would be caught that way again, and open the door to something she shouldn't see.

So the toy business had been a cover up.

She was certain it had been. But why did Luke refuse to believe it? Did it all sound too fantastic?

Abby went down the stairs slowly. Strangely enough, she was no longer frightened. The interior of the building looked just the way Luke must have seen it, a steep flight of stairs leading to a small back room which suggested a very struggling business, if any business at all. It was nothing to get fussed about. Certainly it could suggest nothing sinister.

But it had been important enough for someone, with furious speed, to provide a camouflage.

Or had she imagined the whole thing? Or was she in another building altogether?

On an impulse she went into the dress shop downstairs. The stupid girl there had been no use at all yesterday, but today perhaps she would find the owner in.

There was no one about, and Abby had to ring the bell on the small glass counter. She wondered dispiritedly whether to buy one of the not particularly attractive dresses in return for what information she received. She had her back turned, and was studying a gaudy red and yellow cotton sun dress which made her think of the hot splashes of color in the suburban gardens when someone spoke behind her.

'Can I help you, madam?'

She turned and looked into the curiously over-brilliant eyes of the plump and cosy

136

woman who yesterday had sat primly behind the desk in the room upstairs.

Their sensation of shock was mutual. Abby recovered first.

'So you're Miss Court,' she said. 'I thought you did your sewing at home. Or did your assistant mean you did it upstairs?'

'No, no, you're making a mistake,' the woman said quickly. 'I'm not Miss Court. I've only just started here today. You're the lady who came up yesterday, aren't you? Asking for a cosmetic company.'

'Yes,' Abby said, waiting.

'I suppose I should have told you then, only I didn't think it was your business. But the R. B. Mitchell company has closed. The old man died a few weeks ago. I only stayed on to wind up things. I thought if I didn't say anything I might have made a sale. We hoped to clear out the rest of our stock. There was little enough money in the estate, and the old man left a widow.'

Abby stood looking at her, saying nothing.

'Miss Court was waiting for me to come down here as soon as I could. It's just a coincidence it's today. What were you wanting, madam? A dress? We've a nice range, and Miss Court will make anything to measure.'

'Will she? Could I see her now?'

'I'm afraid you couldn't. She works at home. But I can take your order.'

Oddly enough, for someone so practised in

137

evasions, the woman had a nice face. A little high-colored, and with that strung-up look, but nice and trustworthy.

'So you're really not Miss Court yourself?'

'No, madam. I've just come here, I said. Miss Court's been waiting for me to be free.'

'Why should I believe you?' Abby said.

'I didn't ask you to believe me, madam,' said the woman huffily. 'I didn't ask you to ask me questions. I might add, if you're not looking for a dress, what exactly are you doing?'

The fog was coming down again. What *was* she doing here? This plump, respectable woman obviously had nothing to do with a non-existent cosmetic company or with a lipstick called Galah.

'Actually, I came again to look at your toys,' she said dazedly. 'You remember you said I could get some wholesale if I wanted to.'

'I did say that.'

'But you should have added that yesterday was the last day. Why did you deceive me? I came in here to ask if anyone knew why the room upstairs was always shut.

'Well, that's why,' said the woman briefly. 'It's shut for good now. But there are still a few toys up there. You're welcome to look, if you like. They'll have to be sold somewhere.'

Was this also a deception? At least it was one thing Abby could prove.

'Then will you take me up and show them to me? Now?'

Instantly, before any more strange transformations could be made . . .

'Certainly. Wait till I call Linda. That girl's always off making tea. She'd guzzle it all day. Linda!'

From somewhere in the back the girl with the pale, stupid face appeared.

'Yes, Miss—'

'I'm going to be out for a few minutes. Watch the shop. If Mrs. Frisby calls ask her to wait. I want to see that suit on her myself.' The woman turned to add, as she was following Abby out, 'Miss Court asked me to.'

And that explanation seemed a little belated. For someone who had just begun work in a dress shop, after presumably years of selling toys, she seemed very confident. Quite as confident as the absent proprietress herself . . .

Nevertheless the toys were upstairs. Behind the partition, in the slightly musty-smelling room (it still had the lingering odor Abby had smelled the other day), there were boxes higgledy-piggledy, with their contents spilling out. As if they were being packed to move—or had hastily been dumped there.

'What is the age of the child you want something for? A boy or a girl?'

'A girl of eight. With rather original tastes. I don't think a doll would do at all.'

Abby was finding it difficult to concentrate. She was certain this was the bare room into which she had stumbled accidentally. There was the same narrow window looking on to a well, also the door at the side, now firmly shut. But she couldn't have said whether the walls had been painted this dingy yellow, or whether the floor had been covered with worn linoleum. At the time of seeing the room she had noticed little more than the packing-cases and the subtly menacing face of the man with the flesh-colored hair. And the opening door . . .

Remembering that, her skin prickled.

'Where does that door lead to?' she asked.

'Down a back stairway. Why?'

'I just wondered if you had more things in another room.'

'No, this is all that's left. And not much of a choice. Would the little girl like cut-out books? Or this embroidery set?'

Thinking of Deirdre sitting sewing, Abby smiled.

'I'm afraid not. She's an outdoor child. I'll tell you what I'd like, the toy you had on the counter yesterday. The girl on a swing. It might amuse Deirdre.'

'Deir—'

The woman stopped, and Abby met her over-bright eyes.

'I was just going to say, what an attractive name.'

'You sounded as if it surprised you. Do you know Deirdre Henderson?'

140

'No, I don't know her.'

The woman met her gaze quite levelly. She didn't seem to be lying. Anyway, why should she? If she did know Deirdre, why couldn't she admit it quite safely?

'So you'd like the swing, would you, madam? Wait till I find a box to put it in. It'll be seven and six. Is that all right?'

'Fine, thanks.'

A box was found, and the little figure fitted into it. It was only after she had taken it that Abby realized now Luke and Lola would know she had been back here. But she didn't intend to deny it, anyway. She would admit to Luke that she had broken her promise. And come to no harm . . .

'If that's all you're wanting, madam, I'll have to fly. Linda isn't very reliable in the shop. She's too inexperienced. And don't waste your time coming up again, because after the end of the week this place will be closed for good. You've found it just too late.'

So tomorrow it would be the empty dusty room again. If it *was* the same room . . . Abby felt a slight dizziness. Had she been incredibly wrong, or had an hallucination? The box in her hand containing the girl on the swing, the plump, cosy woman with her too watchful eyes, were the only concrete things. The other must have been hallucination . . .

*   *   *

141

It was half past four. Abby decided to take a taxi to Luke's office in order to get a ride home with him. Before they picked up Lola, since that would be inevitable, she would tell him the latest developments in this perplexing part of the world. She wouldn't make a thing of it. It was nothing to do with her if an old man called R. B. Mitchell had died, or if his middle-aged assistant now turned to dressmaking. It was all rather sad in a cosy kind of way.

But it was not on the dramatic level of the fish-faced man and his threats. How improbable all that seemed now.

With Deirdre's present hanging from one finger by its string, Abby quite light-heartedly went up the stairs to Luke's office. Without admitting it even to herself, she was greatly relieved at being able to avoid that last hour of dusk in the house alone. It was an hour she was coming to dread.

Miss Atkinson sprang up from her typewriter.

'Why, Mrs. Fearon! You didn't say you were coming.'

'Must I?' said Abby.

Miss Atkinson looked put out and disapproving.

'Well, if you want to take a risk on Mr. Fearon being out. And he is.' She must have noticed the change in Abby's face, for she

142

relented. 'But he should be back any minute. He's only gone over to the North Shore for an hour. You'd better wait.'

'Thank you, Miss Atkinson. How's your mother?'

'Only so so. But what can you expect at her age. Seventy-seven next week.'

'Really!' said Abby sympathetically.

Having a frail, elderly mother had developed Miss Atkinson's maternal and managing qualities. She had grown too bossy. Abby wondered how Luke, who was none too patient himself, put up with this. But apparently he liked it. And one had to admit the woman was the loyal kind. She had a heart of gold beneath a waspish exterior. Abby only resented that she always made her feel like a child.

'You going out to dinner again tonight?' Miss Atkinson asked.

So she knew about last night. What didn't she know? She and Lola between them seemed to own more of Luke than Abby did.

Abby made herself answer pleasantly.

'We're going to Deirdre's birthday party. I've just been buying her a present.'

She had wandered into Luke's office, and sat down at his desk, pleased to see that her own photograph was placed prominently, as if he liked to look at it.

There were letters and plans scattered about. She looked at them all lovingly. They

143

were Luke's, and therefore special. She didn't really mind Miss Atkinson with her heart of gold managing Luke's business life.

'That was nasty, that burglary,' called Miss Atkinson.

'Yes, it was.'

'Made you nervous?'

'N-no. Well, yes, it has a little. Luke offered to move if I hated it. But I couldn't be a rabbit like that, could I? Running away. Besides we couldn't afford it. A move's too expensive.'

'Quite right,' said Miss Atkinson, and there seemed to be grudging approval in her voice. She began to clatter at her typewriter.

Abby restlessly fiddled with pens and pencils, then absently pulled open the drawer of Luke's desk.

The first thing she saw was the lipstick.

At first she thought it was the one he had thrown down the rubbish shute, the one Deirdre had given her. Then she realized that it couldn't be. It must be another, made by the same company. Yes, there stamped on the bottom was the name 'Galah'. It seemed to scream at her, like the harsh noise the parrots made.

She held the small gold object in her hand as if it were a snake.

What did Luke know that he had never told her?

She was so absorbed that she didn't hear him come in. Then she scarcely noticed the

144

pleasure in his voice.

'Why, Abby!'

She got up and held out the lipstick.

'I wasn't looking for it. I just happened to see it.'

'It's Lola's.' He hadn't hesitated. But had his eyes given the slightest flicker? Now they looked straight at her with that look of innocence. 'She left it in the car. Don't look so shocked. What on earth are you thinking?'

'How did she come to leave it in the car?'

'Don't ask me. She's always titivating.'

'Why does she have so many lipsticks of this make?'

'So many! This just makes two, doesn't it? After all, Deirdre pinched her other one.'

'And yet neither she nor you know anything about who makes this particular brand. Even the girl in Simpsons hadn't heard of it.'

'Give it to me.' His voice was curt, cold, withdrawn. He meant to tell her nothing at all.

She handed him the lipstick without protest.

'And what other shops did you make enquiries in?'

'Only Simpsons.'

'Abby, for God's sake, why attach such a mystery to an innocent lipstick. Lola doesn't enquire where her firm gets the stuff. But it's so footling a thing. Can't you see?'

'The thing that isn't footling,' said Abby stubbornly, 'is that you should have another woman's lipstick in your desk. Why didn't you

145

leave it in the car and give it to Lola tonight?'

'Don't ask me! I just automatically removed it. Perhaps I'm tidy-minded. Now can you keep quiet for ten minutes while I sign this mail. Then we can get away and so can Miss Atkinson. What are you doing in town anyway?'

But now Abby knew that she wasn't going to show him Deirdre's present or tell him where she had been. She hated herself for that. But some dreadful compulsion kept her silent. Together with Lola, Luke would have to look at the little figure on the swing and remember where it came from. And she would watch their faces . . .

CHAPTER TEN

A movement in the mirror caught her eye. Abby turned sharply to see the pale, sly face at the window. Deirdre was watching again.

She wished she had drawn the curtains, but it was too late now. Resignedly she went over and opened the window. Deirdre, already in the blue party dress, grinned at her unashamedly.

'I just wanted to see what you were wearing.'

'Haven't you been told it's rude to look in other people's windows?'

'I have something to tell you,' said Deirdre sulkily.

'Well, what is it?'

'Mummy's been talking on the telephone to my father again.'

'Deirdre, how do you know it's your father?'

'She calls him Reg. I don't know. I just think he's my father.' Deirdre turned away with studied nonchalance. 'Anyway, he's not coming to the party because she said, "Don't you dare show up tonight." When she stopped talking Uncle Milton said, "I'm still not sure you can trust him," and Mummy said, "I am," and went away.'

'You mean she can't trust Reg?'

'I don't know. Either him or Luke.'

Abby leaned out into the chill evening air. 'Deirdre, you're telling lies again. How could she possibly mean Luke? What's he got to do with this man called Reg?'

In the dim light Deirdre's pale face had a look of unchildish amusement.

'Because Mummy said when she got to the door, "Anyway, I want him, so that's that." And she'd just told Reg to stay away. So it must have been Luke. It's always Luke she's hanging around. She's done it for months. She's soppy about him.'

'Deirdre, don't you dare say that again! It's not true, and you're no friend of mine if you talk like that. Besides, what a way to behave, looking in people's windows, listening to telephone conversations, and then repeating them.'

Abruptly the child colored. Her mouth went into a straight, hard line. Then she flung out,

'If you hate me you don't have to come to my party!' and turned and ran off, a ghostly shape in her pale blue dress in the dusk.

Abby bit her lip. She shouldn't have been so sharp. The child was intolerable, but she was also a deeply sensitive and much too easily hurt person being perverted by her environment. With love and understanding one could find something worthwhile there.

With love and understanding . . . Whoever had enough of those two things?

Abby pulled the curtains slowly, wondering

148

what had made her put on her rose-patterned silk dress which instinctively she knew Deirdre would like best of any in her wardrobe, and why she was going to such an odious child's party. In the hall the telephone rang. Luke, who had been in the living-room finishing some work he had brought home from the office, answered it.

'Abby, it's for you.'

'Who is it?' she asked, hearing her voice quite normal, in spite of the coolness between them.

'I don't know. Some female.'

She went to pick up the receiver. She heard the voice, rather husky, saying, 'Is that Mrs. Fearon?' She didn't recognize it, although it sounded vaguely familiar.

'Yes, this is she.'

She was aware that Luke was standing behind her.

'You know that thing you were asking me about this afternoon? I'd go to Rose Bay, if I were you.'

Before she could say anything at all, the receiver clicked. Her caller had hung up.

'That was a short conversation,' said Luke. 'Who was it?'

Why was he standing there watching and listening? Had he become one of the watchers, too? Please heaven, no! But again caution prevented Abby from telling him what had just happened, and that tomorrow she would go to the seaside suburb with the lovely name and make another search for that mysterious cosmetic company. For her caller must have been the woman in the George Street store where she had made enquiries.

'Darling, I don't stand and listen in to your telephone conversations,' she said, with light reproof.

'You're welcome to. Your friend hadn't much to say. I've never known a woman of so few words.'

He was smiling. His eyes were cool and wary.

'Oh, it was just a shopgirl who was trying to get me something. She has told me where I can probably get it.

'Get what?'

'The kind of girdle I like, if you must know,' said Abby exasperatedly. 'You'd have thought it would be easy enough to get. Any decent shop in London would have it. But here, nobody knows anything!'

She was hiding her agitation by giving vent to her homesickness and prejudice against this strange, too bright, too brash city.

'All right, we're a nation of morons,' said Luke. He seemed to have relaxed. 'You're looking very charming. Is this all for Deirdre?'

'That little monster!' Abby exclaimed.

Luke gave his hearty laugh.

'What, is she in this general hate, too? Am I, also? Are you still worrying about that

150

ridiculous lipstick?'

'Luke, what *is* Lola to you?' Abby burst out. 'I must know.'

His face went hard. She had known it would. But this was something that must be brought into the open.

'She's a good friend, as are all her family. Nothing more.'

'I don't believe you,' said Abby flatly. 'I've tried to, but I can't.'

'I'm sorry. I'm telling you the truth.'

'Perhaps it is the truth as far as you're concerned, but it isn't for Lola. She's crazy about you. Even her own daughter can see that.'

He frowned angrily. 'Good heavens, Abby, you're not believing that child's inventions! She's the biggest little liar in Sydney.'

'Then who is Reg?' Abby countered.

'I haven't the least idea.'

'Deirdre says he's her father, and her mother is always ringing him up. If he is her father, why do we never see him? Why is he kept in the background? Especially, why is he kept out of your sight?'

Luke made an impatient movement.

'Really, darling, you talk of Deirdre always sticking her nose into someone else's business. What about yours—charming as it is? You've already had me on one wild goose chase. So don't let's embark on another. Whoever this Reg is, he's nothing to do with us. Any more

151

than old Jock down there, or that other fellow you talked of, the ridiculous fish-faced man. Forget it, can't you? You're my wife, and Lola's nothing but a friend. How can I prove that to you?'

'By not seeing her any more,' said Abby calmly.

'Oh, really, darling. One's next door neighbors. We can't be that uncivilized.' He didn't care what he was doing to her, his voice was too brisk and impersonal, as if he were talking to some foolish, bird-brained woman in trouble. 'And anyway I've promised to go on this kangaroo shoot this week-end. For Milton's sake, poor devil. Surely you can understand that. How would you like to be condemned to a wheel chair?'

And be stuck helplessly and ignominiously in the toilet when a mischievous child wheeled your means of conveyance away . . . Abby had a moment of compunction.

'I'm sorry about that, but what can I do?'

'Only be reasonably friendly,' said Luke. 'By the way, you won't want to stay here alone for those two days. Will you have Miss Atkinson to stay? Or go up to Mrs. Moffatt? She'd be delighted to have you.'

Abby thought of the two alternatives and shuddered. She thought of the third, that would be to stay here alone, listening to every sound, thinking she heard footsteps prowling, waiting for the telephone to ring . . .

'I suppose I'll have to come with you,' she said.

'I don't think so. You'd hate it.' His denial was too quick. It hid alarm. Milton and Mary would be in their car, the special one that allowed room for Milton's chair to be wheeled in and then left room only for the driver and, at a pinch, one more person. So Luke would take his car, and Lola. Of course Abby would be the odd one out. And yet, not five minutes ago, Luke had been protesting that Lola was merely a friend, a 'civilized' friend.

Abby's hurt was too heavy and forlorn for tears.

'I couldn't bear to shoot a kangaroo or anything else. But I'd still like to come. I've never seen the outback.'

'It's desolate and empty and eerie. Especially at this time of year. You wouldn't like it at all.' Luke glanced at his watch. 'Isn't it time we were going if we're to blow out candles, or whatever it is?'

'Luke, why have you changed so much?'

She saw his eyes flicker, caught a momentary naked look, a look almost of agony that surely she must have imagined. Then the mask was down again, and he was saying with an air of surprise,

'Changed? Have I? But you'd never seen me in my own surroundings, had you? This is how I am as an Australian. If you don't like me, it's bad luck, isn't it?' He gave his young, charming smile that didn't touch his eyes. For no reason at all she was hearing those words he had whispered on their wedding night. 'Try to understand . . .'

But it was beyond her. She gave up.

*   *   *

Deirdre opened the square parcel, and shrieked with pleasure. She tipped the little figure with her finger, and as it swung back and forth she said delightedly,

'Isn't it cute! Mummy, isn't it cute! Look, if I push her hard enough she stands on her head.'

Surely enough, the toy figure, in a flurry of white petticoats, did stand on her head for one paralysed moment, then abruptly rocketed backwards to swing dizzily.

Again Abby felt as if she herself were swinging upside down. For no one was watching Deirdre displaying spontaneous pleasure for the first time. They were all looking at Abby, the giver of the present.

And they all knew. Somehow she was certain they did. Or else they had caught Lola's and Luke's tension. Even the little Christmas-tree figure of Mrs. Moffatt was still, her fingers no longer fiddling with her bedizened jewellery.

Then Lola said casually, 'Didn't we see that toy somewhere yesterday?' and if it hadn't

154

been for the paralysed moment of stillness that had caught them, just as it had caught the miniature girl on the swing, one wouldn't have realized anything was wrong.

'Yes, at that place in Kings Cross,' Abby answered, just as calmly. 'I liked it then, remember? I thought I'd go back and buy it for Deirdre when I knew it was her birthday.'

'And—everything was all right?' said Lola.

Abby made herself look at Luke. She had to know finally whose side he was on, hers, or this strange family's, with their stranger secrets. But his face was expressionless, except for a darkened look in his eyes. It could have been caused by anger with her for breaking her promise. Or it could have been anxiety. At least, it wasn't fear. He wouldn't be afraid. Pride stirred in her, and she had to fight to remain as calm as Lola.

'Perfectly all right. At least, not altogether, because old Mr. Mitchell had died. It was rather a coincidence, wasn't it? And the woman who was in his office now works for Miss Court, the dressmaker. In fact, I wondered for a minute if she were Miss Court.'

'Don't be silly, Abby. She'd been with that toy outfit for years, obviously. It was lucky for her to step into another job so quickly. But she said she was expecting the old man to die, didn't she?'

'Are we talking about an anonymous woman

155

or this completely fascinating toy,' said Milton in his clipped, tense voice. 'Does it matter where Abby found it? Obviously Deirdre likes it, and that's quite an achievement for Abby.'

He smiled in the way he could, with deliberate charm, a charm that even though rarely used must have kept Mary in helpless subjection to him.

'It's a different sort of thing,' Deirdre said, her face cupped in her hands as she stared at the little swinging figure. 'It's not useful. I hate useful presents.'

'Well, that's a compliment to me!' said Lola. 'I thought you quite liked your new dress last night.'

'And I gave you that pretty necklace,' said Mrs. Moffatt, tinkling and chinking. 'You'd hardly call that useful, but you seemed disappointed with it.'

'Oh, beads!' said Deirdre.

'Deirdre, that's rude to your grandmother,' said Lola crossly. 'You loved your necklace. You know you did. You loved all your presents. Even if Abby's is the most original. Fancy you going back to that place, Abby. I thought it gave you the jimjams.'

'Not that one,' said Abby. 'It couldn't be more ordinary, could it? It's the Rose Bay Cosmetic Company that I'm still trying to find. And that seems to have disappeared into thin air.' 'Go to Rose Bay' the husky feminine voice on the telephone had said. So there was such a company. It had merely moved—very quickly. But she couldn't tell anybody this interesting fact, or else the company was likely to move again. And she had to find it. It was most urgent to do so. Because now her own husband was implicated.

'If it ever existed,' said Lola.

'We didn't hear much about this,' Milton said, moving restlessly in his chair. 'In fact, you're all talking double Dutch as far as Mary and I are concerned. Why must you find this place, Abby?'

'Just to prove I didn't imagine it,' said Abby. 'It's not much fun being threatened by strange men, but it's even less fun thinking you've imagined the whole thing. I'd need to go to a psychiatrist, wouldn't I?' She laughed easily, willing Luke to laugh with her. 'It must be something Australia has done to me.'

'You haven't seen Australia yet,' said Milton. 'Only Sydney. You might as well go to the States and see nothing but New York. I think you'd better come with us on this trip we're planning. At least you'll see something of the country.'

Another stone had been dropped into this murky pool. Milton's suggestion was obviously completely unexpected, and also unwelcome.

'But Abby is going to stay with Deirdre and me,' Mrs. Moffatt protested.

Lola sprang up to light a cigarette. She had her slim back to the room.

157

'She hates the thought of shooting kangaroos. She'd loathe it.' She turned, and her eyes, curiously golden, held Abby's. 'Wouldn't you, honey?'

Abby lifted her chin. 'I was telling Luke I'd like to come. Wasn't I, darling? I expect I will loathe it, but if I'm to live in this country I ought to do these things, oughtn't I?'

Luke spoke at last. 'Nonsense! It's not a thing women do at all. And you would hate it, Abby. I've told you.'

'I think she'd like to see the outback,' said Milton persuasively. 'She'd find it exciting, even if not the height of comfort. You're not being very gallant, are you, Luke? Leaving your wife out of an interesting expedition?'

Something flashed in Luke's face. He stubbed out his cigarette with exaggerated firmness.

'I think you're underestimating my wife. If she intends to do a thing she does it.'

He was referring to her broken promise. She didn't miss the undertone of bitterness in his voice. It was all right for him to deceive her, but not her him. Her unhappiness settled more heavily on her.

'I don't like being left out of things,' she said frankly. 'You all seemed to have made arrangements for me, just like a package to be stored. I didn't like it.'

Milton had wheeled his chair over to her. For a moment his long, pale hand, unexpectedly strong, pressed hers. She tried not to draw back.

'You're perfectly right, Abby. Don't let Luke keep you on ice.' He laughed, a deep masculine roar, taking the sting out of the joke. 'Eh, Luke?'

Luke's mouth tightened. Abby expected him to lose his temper in the sharp devastating way he could. She held her breath, hoping he would, praying that the hold these people had on him wasn't that strong.

But apparently it was. For after a moment he shrugged and said lightly, 'Okay. You win, Abby. But don't blame us if you hate every minute of it.'

'Well, what a party this is!' Deirdre put in peevishly. 'You all just talk, talk, talk. Why don't we play games or something?'

'Or have some drinks,' said Lola. 'That's a far better idea. That's what we need. And Deirdre, honey, I'm bringing your cake in for you to cut, and after that you go to bed.'

'Bed! At my party!'

'Sweetie, you'll have had your party. Look at the time! It's ten o'clock. And school tomorrow. And no sick turns in the morning, remember. So be a poppet and behave.'

'I couldn't go to sleep,' Deirdre muttered. 'You'll all be walking about. I told you I never go to sleep when people walk in the night.'

'We've got a ghost now, you see,' said Lola. 'You and Deirdre, Abby, make a good pair.'

159

She laughed good-naturedly, and began pouring drinks.

Getting off her chair, Deirdre began to stump up and down.

'Like that,' she said.

Milton's brows tightened. His face looked white and bad-tempered.

'Lola, this child is beyond a joke. I've told you, she'll have to go to boarding school. It's not only her habit of telling lies, it's this impudence. She'll have to be taught manners.'

Old Mrs. Moffatt made a move, her thin hands twining frantically among her beads.

'This is still my house, Milton. I won't have Deirdre sent away if—' Her long, brown eyes held her son-in-law's for a moment, then slid away. Her lips trembled. She gave a quick look of appeal at Mary who smiled faintly, saying nothing. Mary was a rabbit, completely dominated by her husband.

'Don't get fussed, mother,' said Lola briskly. 'You know Milton's perfectly right about Deirdre. She's got out of hand. So long as I have to work I can't give enough time to her, and she twists you round her little finger. Don't you, hon?' She turned to Deirdre. 'Go and bring your cake in. It's all ready. And then off to bed with you, or goodness knows what Abby will think of such a quarrelsome family.'

She hadn't said 'and Luke'. For apparently Luke knew well enough what the Moffatt family was like, and didn't mind.

'And here's your drink, Mother. Abby? A dry martini? I warn you, I mix them the American way. Oh God, let's be gay!'

She was so attractive with her sun-burned face and thick, careless, fair hair and lithe body. But her mysterious husband hadn't come to Deirdre's party. Because he had been told to stay away?

Abby sipped her drink, then swallowed it quickly, resolving, like Lola, that the only thing to do was to be gay. For worrying achieved nothing whatever.

Deirdre, endeavouring to hide her pleasure under her casual, deadpan manner, blew out the candles on her cake, and cut it with grave attention. Then, at her mother's repeated injunctions, she at last went upstairs to bed.

But when a few minutes later, the telephone rang and Lola went to answer it, Deirdre had obviously got there first, for Lola could be heard exclaiming, 'Give it to me at once! I've told you you're not to do that. You're to call somebody to come. Now off upstairs!'

Abby put her glass down—the strong drink had made her feel not so much gay as completely indifferent to what anyone thought—and said that she was going upstairs to say good night to Deirdre.

'After all, it is her birthday,' she said. 'And she's only had us being scratchy with each other.'

'She adored your present, dear,' said Mrs.

Moffatt. 'But I agree with Milton, she is a problem.'

'She's lonely,' said Abby. 'I know. I used to feel like that myself.'

Deirdre was sitting up in bed playing with the little figure on the swing. As she swung it backwards and forwards, she was chanting to herself, 'Rose Bay's a place, not a lady. A place, not a lady. Oh, hullo, Abby. I'm too old to be kissed good night.'

'Why are you saying that about Rose Bay?' Abby asked.

'Someone on the telephone said, "Is that Rose Bay?"' Deirdre began to giggle. 'Do I look like Rose Bay? Houses, shops, sand, sea, swings. Look, even swings . . .'

She swung the figure madly. She was very overexcited, and talking nonsense.

'You'd better go to sleep,' said Abby. 'It was a lovely party. You cut the cake beautifully.'

'But my father didn't come.'

'You made that up about your father, didn't you?'

For once, the sharp, unswerving eyes were bewildered.

'I don't know,' said Deirdre. 'I don't know.'

Impulsively Abby stooped and kissed the suddenly forlorn face.

'Go to sleep, darling. You're tired.'

Deirdre lay back obediently and Abby switched off the light.

'Abby, are you up there with Deirdre?'

called Lola sharply. 'Come down and get another drink. For goodness sake, the party's scarcely started.'

'In a moment,' answered Abby. 'What was that, Deirdre?'

'Do you think it was Miss Rose Bay he wanted? Miss Rose Bay. What a name!'

But something to turn over in one's mind, Abby thought, as she went into Mrs. Moffatt's room to tidy herself. The possibility that Rose Bay was a woman . . .

She sat peering into the age-dimmed mirror, thinking that compared with Lola she did look too fragile and pink and white. If there was anyone in this house called Rose, it was a name more suited to herself. Lola was a golden tiger-lily, Mrs. Moffatt like the brown, Australian boronia with the heavy scent. Mary was nothing . . .

Still lost in thought she went slowly down the stairs, not realizing how quiet she was until she heard the voices in the hall, Lola's and Luke's.

Luke was saying, 'It's just as important for me as for you. I've got to make money, too. I've got a wife now.'

'And you will buy her expensive flowers,' Lola said, laughing without kindness.

Their voices drifted away. Abby stood quite still, the pain sharp in her heart.

So she was too expensive. The flowers yesterday had been necessary to keep her

163

happy, to keep her quiet . . .

CHAPTER ELEVEN

Abby stood on the patio a moment looking over the moonlit river. Jock's boat lay in darkness, and a welcome silence. The cool breeze rustled the pungas with a gentle melancholy sound. Abby breathed deeply, trying to clear her head and ease her overwhelming tiredness.

She was aware of Luke coming to stand beside her. She spoke without turning. 'I'm not sorry I broke my promise about going up to the Cross, but it didn't do any good. I only got more mixed up.'

He spoke gently, 'It doesn't matter, Abby.'

But now it was too late for gentleness. She turned on him.

'And I don't know what it is you and Lola are up to, but if it's just something you're doing for money, I'll never forgive you. Never! And now I don't want to talk any more.'

She left him standing there in the cool moonlight. From weariness and the lingering effect of the martinis, she was more than half asleep when he came to bed.

Abby woke in the morning to find Luke fully dressed sitting on the side of the bed. The sun was streaming in. She could hear the wind blowing and the pigeons cooing in the gum trees. It was obviously very late.

'Hullo, darling,' said Luke. 'I let you sleep.'

Abby started up.

'But what happened to the alarm? What time is it?'

'Ten o'clock.'

'Ten! Why aren't you at the office?'

He laughed. With one finger he delicately sketched a half circle beneath her eyes.

'You have shadows there. You're tired. I hadn't noticed. So today I make amends and look after you.'

'What about your clients and your appointments? What's Miss Atkinson saying?'

'I don't know what she's saying, but she's coping. She'd better be. I rang her an hour ago while you were still asleep. She sent you her love.'

For one moment Abby let the bliss, like warm sunlight, soak through her. Then her brain began to function and she said warily,

'What is all this V.I.P. treatment for? I'm not ill.'

'No, but you're overstrained. I didn't realize how much until last night. I was very worried about you.'

'You mean about my fancies,' said Abby tiredly. She had known the warm dream would dissolve.

'About you, my sweet. I'm quite attached to you. Remember?'

Abby sat up, pushing back the blankets.

'It can't be this late. I must get dressed. Yes,

I know you're attached to me. It's a thing that happens when the marriage service is read over you. We took each other, plus friends and relations, plus worries and secrets and hallucinations and bad tempers, the lot.'

Luke remained calm, a little amused.

'Abby, that's not like you. Being cynical.'

Abby stood on the floor in her nightdress. She rubbed her eyes and pushed back her hair. She was still tired, irrecoverably tired. She didn't want to begin thinking.

But the day had started long ago, and if one went on living one had to begin new days.

'Then what are you going to do? Look after me all day?'

'I was planning to take you shopping. You'll need suitable clothes for the week-end.'

Abby looked surprised.

'Surely it isn't a social occasion.'

Luke moved impatiently, losing his unnatural forbearance at last.

'Of course it isn't a social occasion. Wait until you see the pub where we'll spend the night. But have you got walking shoes? A thick skirt and jumper? Some sort of heavy jacket? No, of course you haven't. You came out here prepared for tropical weather. It can be pretty cold in the outback at nights at this time of year. Anyway, you'll want those sort of clothes sometime. We might as well get them all. Then I'll take you somewhere interesting for lunch.'

'How sweet of you, Luke,' Abby said

mechanically, knowing with certainty that he only wanted to keep her under his eye. He didn't intend that today she should do any more awkward investigating.

'Well, look a little more enthusiastic,' Luke said. 'Can you be ready in half an hour or so? I'll make some coffee while you have your bath.'

'Have you fed the kookies?'

'Yes. Greedy brutes.'

'What about Lola? How did she get to work?'

'By ferry, I imagine. I told her you weren't well and I was staying with you.'

Abby exclaimed indignantly, 'What a thing to say. I'm perfectly well.'

Luke took her and faced her to the mirror.

'Look at that face! Like something the cat brought home.'

'Luke!'

'Isn't that true?'

Abby rubbed her pale cheeks. She knew, unhappily, that for once Lola would have caught the ferry without grumbling. She would agree that Abby should be kept under supervision.

'All right, be my jailer,' she said.

Luke spun her round, shaking her severely.

'Abby, stop that idiotic talk! Your jailer! My God!'

Abby began to laugh uncertainly, nearer to tears.

168

'All right, Luke. I promise not to ask questions. But whatever you and Lola are up to, you can't hide it from me forever, can you? I can only be kept quiet with flowers and expensive lunches for a certain time.'

His face had darkened furiously. She saw his hands clench. Then he turned abruptly and went out of the room without saying anything at all. Without even making a denial . . .

She bathed and dressed and carefully made up her face so that it looked more alive, and healthy. Indeed, the face looking back at her from the mirror could almost pass for that of an attractive and happy young bride. She went into the living-room and drank the coffee Luke had prepared, and watched him go through to the kitchen to wash the cups. His tall, lean figure at the sink, solemnly doing the unaccustomed work, quickened a pain in her that she could scarcely bear. It was a happy domestic scene that had got irreparably out of focus. She sprang up and went outdoors into the fresh morning sunshine.

Then she saw the geraniums she had planted yesterday were drooping. But when she went to get the watering can Luke said impatiently, 'What are you doing? You haven't time for that. Jock can water the garden. I'll call him up. He can also keep an eye on the place while we're away.'

'That old scoundrel!' Abby said.

'There you are, you see,' said Luke. 'You

169

have this habit of thinking everybody's a scoundrel or crooked. What's old Jock done to deserve it? Or Lola? Or those perfectly innocent people you've got mixed up with in Kings Cross? Or even I? What's happened to you, Abby? You didn't used to be like this. Suspicious, fanciful, nervous.'

Now he was confusing her again, turning her thoughts upside down.

'Everything hasn't been fancy. The burglar, for instance—'

But could it be herself, and not Luke, who had changed?

'Darling, now you're looking white and miserable again. Get your hat on and let's get out of here.'

Abby said that apart from buying the things Luke suggested she would like to look at that girdle in Simpsons, the one the shop assistant had rung up about. So would Luke wait downstairs while she did so.

Luke looked at her sharply. Was he suspicious again? But he said quite easily, 'All right. But don't be all day. I thought we'd go out to one of the bays for lunch.'

'Which one?'

'Any one you like. The famous Rose Bay, if you like.'

'What fun,' said Abby. ('Go to Rose Bay,' the woman had said. In a moment she would have found out why . . .)

She took the lift up to the third floor in case

170

Luke should have thought she wasn't going to the lingerie department, then slipped quickly across the carpeted room and down the stairs. The cosmetic counter was a long way from where she had left Luke, and the store crowded enough for her to be unobserved. She had purposely worn an inconspicuous gray hat and suit.

The same woman, chic and smiling, was behind the counter. Abby leaned across conspiratorially.

'I'm Mrs. Fearon, do you remember? I wanted to thank you for ringing me last night. But why did you tell me to go to Rose Bay?'

'Mrs. Fearon?' said the woman in a puzzled voice. 'Did I ring you?'

'Yes! Yes, don't you remember? About the Rose Bay Cosmetic Company.'

'You came in yesterday. Of course. But I didn't ring you, Mrs. Fearon. I couldn't find out anything about that company. Our chief buyer doesn't know it. I'm sorry I can't help you.'

The fog again, blinding, breathless.

'Then if you didn't ring me, who did?'

'I'm sure I don't know. Have you been asking in other places?'

Only in Kings Cross. And no one there would ring her. No one knew who she was. Unless . . .

'Thank you, anyway,' said Abby, trying to speak calmly. 'Is there a telephone I could

171

use?'

'There's one at the door. Have you got four pennies?'

'Yes, I have.' With trembling fingers, Abby checked. Where was Luke? Not anywhere near the telephone, she hoped.

She was certain she slipped into the box unobserved. Then she had to search through the book for the number. Court, dressmaker. The cosy woman with the too bright eyes. She would recognize that voice again, even if a little deliberately husky, as a disguise.

Here it was. Miss M. Court, dressmaker, Kings Cross. Abby memorised the number, and dialled.

After a few moments of ringing a laconic voice said, 'Hullo.'

'Is that Miss Court?'

'Not speaking. This is her shop.'

Abby recognized the voice of the moronic girl.

'Then is Miss Court there? I want to speak to her.'

'She isn't in yet. She might be in later.'

Abby clenched her fingers impatiently.

'Can I ring her at her house? Can you give me her number?'

'Well—if it's urgent. I suppose you could. She doesn't like getting calls at home.'

'Just give me her number,' said Abby crisply.

It was fortunate she had another four pennies, a miracle, almost. She was able to dial the number the girl had given her and wait, scarcely breathing, for the answer.

At last it came, a husky far-off voice.

'Yes? Who is it?'

'This is Mrs. Fearon speaking. I think you rang me last night. I wanted to know—'

'Mrs. Fearon. Never heard the name. Who put you on to me? I was just taking a nap—'

The voice was querulous, very old.

It was a mistake. Abby persevered hopelessly, 'Then did someone else in your house ring me? Could you find out? It's important.'

'It's no use ringing me, dear. I don't make dresses now. I have arthritis in my hands. I'm eighty-six. If you ring—' Abruptly the far-away quavering voice ceased, the receiver clicked. Someone had put it down firmly. Someone had interrupted.

Now she had a telephone number and no address. She would have to ring the stupid girl again for the address. But she had no more pennies. And it was twenty minutes since she had left Luke. He would be coming up to find her. She didn't dare risk any more time. Later, given an opportunity, she must ring that girl again for the address, and then go and call on old Miss Court, aged eighty-six, and suffering from arthritis so badly that she couldn't possibly have made the droopy, black lace dress, or any other. Or, indeed, taken any interest in obtaining the services of the cosy

173

woman from the toy shop upstairs . . .

Abby flew up the stairs to the first floor, then queued to get into the descending lift. No more than a little flushed, she emerged to find Luke standing almost exactly where she had left him. He looked bored and impatient, and instantly noticed that she didn't carry a parcel.

'All that time for nothing,' she said breathlessly. 'Nothing fitted me properly.'

He was only a little sceptical.

'I wouldn't have thought you'd be so difficult to fit.'

Abby tucked her arm through his. 'Quote "The basis of good dressing is the foundation garment". Unquote. Can we lunch now? I'm hungry.'

The idea had come to her that the old woman with the die-away voice was Rose Bay. Age and infirmity had brought the business to an end, but in some unexplained way she still exerted a sinister influence and pursued some mysterious activity.

As Luke had suggested, they did lunch in Rose Bay, a charming and innocent place which Abby now had no desire to explore. The clues were leading away from here, after all. When, after lunch, Luke suggested a drive round the coast, she acquiesced quite willingly. It meant, of course, that he was not going to let her out of his sight, and that she could do no more about Miss Court today. It seemed, indeed, as if the matter would have to wait until after their week-end in the country. But perhaps a breathing space might be a good idea.

First, said Luke, they would go up and take a look at the Gap. On a sunny day it wasn't sinister. It was only during a storm, or at night, with the jagged rocks looking immense, that it was frightening.

'Especially if you haven't a head for heights,' said Luke, and seemed to be waiting for Abby to tell him how her head was in such places.

'Wait till we get there and I'll tell you how I feel,' she said lightly.

The wind was fierce on the cliff tops. When Luke stopped the car and opened the door, it swooped in, catching Abby's breath.

He laughed. 'Hang on to your hair.'

She scrambled out and followed him up the well-worn path to the edge of the cliff. There was nobody about. The rocks shone white in the sun, and beneath them, an immense way down, a sheer fall, crawled the sea, blue-veined and wrinkled.

'Impressive?' Abby heard Luke shouting to her.

She nodded, the wind blowing her hair in her eyes.

'Come over here,' called Luke. 'You can see further.'

She stepped over rocks and boulders to reach his side. He gripped her arm. A sudden feeling of exhilaration filled her. It was like standing on a mountain top, high and clean and windy. For a moment nothing else intruded. There was the magnificent view, and the two of them alone, not being pulled apart by private suspicions and fears.

'It's wonderful,' said Abby.

Luke smiled at her. He looked happy. She always remembered that in that instant he looked happy.

But there was a burr caught in the top of her shoe, pricking her, and she stooped to pick it off. The wind came in a sudden vicious gust, and somehow, it was impossible to say how, she lost her balance. The dizzy height had affected her head, after all. Luke had warned her that it might.

She was aware of a violent swinging together of cliff and sky and sea, and then Luke had dragged her upright, shouting, 'Abby! For God's sake, be careful!'

Upright again, she clung to him, gasping.

'I lost my balance. I shouldn't have stooped.'

'Did you hurt yourself? Let's get away from the edge. I shouldn't have let you come so close.'

His voice was harsh with fright. It was she who had to reassure him.

'I've grazed my arm. That's all. It's this wind. Let's get back to the car.'

'Yes, let's. I said this place wasn't sinister by daylight. But I believe it is. People die here.'

'But by their own will, not by accident,' Abby said practically. She was able to laugh now, recovering from her fright. 'Anyway, I don't suppose I'd have gone far. I wasn't that near the edge.'

Luke opened the door of the car and helped her in. When he was in himself he suddenly took her in his arms, in a violent and painful embrace.

'Oh, Abby!' he said. 'Oh, Abby!'

A car had pulled up behind them, and other people were climbing out into the windy treachery of the day. Luke took his arms away.

'Sorry. It is a bit public.'

He took a cigarette out and lit it. Abby noticed that his hands trembled slightly.

'I believe you got a worse fright than I did.'

He turned on her roughly. 'What did you expect me to do? Laugh? To see you rolling down that monstrous slope.'

'Luke, it didn't happen.'

'No, it didn't.' He relaxed a little, drawing deeply on his cigarette. 'It was my fault, wanting to impress you with the view. I do a lot of crazy things. You must have noticed.'

'Yes,' said Abby soberly. 'I don't know about crazy. But you do things I don't understand.'

She was suddenly remembering Lola saying, 'You have an expensive wife,' and the hurt still lingered. Though not so deeply, with this strangely penitent Luke beside her.

'I've been strung-up lately,' Luke said. 'Too

177

much work, troublesome clients. Things will straighten out soon. Very soon.' He seemed to be making her another promise. 'We'll both be better after this week-end away.'

Did a search for kangaroos provide some special panacea? Abby was content to believe it. She, too, recovered from her inner trembling and relaxed.

CHAPTER TWELVE

Deirdre hung on the car door as Luke stowed in the guns and luggage. When he went back into the house for something she said matter-of-factly, 'I suppose this is when I'll be killed. While you're away.'

'What nonsense you talk,' said Abby. It was early morning and chilly. She wore the thick skirt and sweater she had bought yesterday, and was still cold.

'This isn't nonsense,' said Deirdre. 'He's probably only waiting until I'm alone.'

'Who, for goodness' sake?'

'The man who walks at night. I told you about him.' Deirdre's gaze was reproachful. She had expected more serious attention from Abby than from the rest of her family.

'Do you read a lot?' Abby asked. 'Or watch television.'

'Oh, yes. Sometimes.'

'It gives you ideas, doesn't it? Anyway, why should you, a child, be killed?'

'Because I know too much.'

Abby kept her face solemn.

'Such as what?'

'Well—things.'

'You mean about this person walking at night. If you really think someone does that, why don't you look and see who it is?'

Deirdre's eyes slid away. It was then, with a shocked feeling, that Abby believed her. For the child was scared stiff. All her aggressive casualness was to hide her shame at her fear.

'Some time I will,' she muttered.

'Deirdre, get off that door,' said Luke, coming out. 'You're no lightweight.'

'Luke, Deirdre's bothered about those footsteps she thinks she hears at night,' Abby said. 'Is it all right to go and leave her with her grandmother?'

Luke patted Deirdre's shoulder.

'Not a thing to worry about. I promise you. Anyway, I've asked Jock to keep an eye on both places.'

'Jock!'

'I know you don't trust him, but give a chap like that responsibility and he takes it very seriously. He'll make a fine watchdog.'

Luke smiled at Deirdre and she, catching the confidence in his voice, grinned back. He did speak with confidence, too—as if he knew what he was talking about.

But there was no opportunity to say more, for Lola had come out carrying her bag.

'I'm coming in your car, Luke. Do you mind, Abby? It's more comfortable than Milton's. His chair takes up all the room.'

'Of course,' said Abby calmly.

Old Mrs. Moffatt appeared, waving frantically from the terrace.

'Good-bye Abby and Luke, take care of

yourselves. Deirdre, come and get your breakfast. Bring us back a kangaroo skin, you two. Milton and Mary are just starting. It's going to be a nice day. Deirdre and I will go on a ferry ride or something. Deirdre, love, you're out there in that thin dress. It's still nippy in the mornings, isn't it? Take care, Abby. Come back safely. So many accidents nowadays . . .'

The monologue ceased. As usual, the old lady's conversation was like a tangled skein of wool, following many directions.

'Honestly!' said Lola. 'She never runs out of words. Run along, honey.' She gave Deirdre a push. 'Get your breakfast. And mind what Gran says.'

'You two girls have a nice time,' said Luke.

'A nice time! Just by ourselves!' But Deirdre grinned back spunkily, and Abby found herself blinking away tears. Honestly, she wasn't getting fond of the intolerable child, was she? With her impudence and her inquisitiveness and her lies?

'They will be all right, won't they?'

'Mother and Deirdre!' said Lola in astonishment. 'Good heavens, yes. We often leave them for a weekend. After all, there hasn't been a man in that house for long enough, except Milton, and poor darling, you can hardly count him.'

'Then who does Deirdre think she hears walking at night?'

Lola sighed.

'Don't come up with Deirdre's fantasies, please. Not at this hour of the morning. She doesn't hear a sound. She sleeps like a log, as all children do.'

'Then what's she scared of?' Abby asked bluntly.

'Deirdre scared! My dear, she's as tough as they come. If she's made you think she's scared she's a better actress than even I thought.'

'She's all right, Abby,' said Luke. 'Don't fuss.'

'I don't think Abby knows much about exhibitionist children,' said Lola. 'They'll say anything for attention, you know. Milton's right. Deirdre will have to go to boarding school and learn not to be the center of attention.'

'I'd have called her an introvert, rather than an extrovert,' Abby maintained.

'Deirdre an introvert! Oh, good Lord, no. Not with me as her mother.'

'What about her father?'

'I'd rather not talk about him, if you don't mind, Abby. But if you're looking for where Deirdre gets her gift for making up fantasies, that's the direction you look.'

'When are you expecting him back in Australia?'

'In his own time. He follows his own sweet will. And if I'm waiting for him, he'll be lucky.'

'Deirdre seems to think he's here now.'

182

Lola made an impatient exclamation.

'There you are! Doesn't that prove what I've just been telling you! You can't believe a word she says. Can you, Luke? You know.'

'She's quite a character,' said Luke non-committally. 'Are we supposed to be tailing Mary and Milton? If so, we'd better get moving.'

*   *   *

It was late in the afternoon that Abby saw her first flock of galahs. They had been searching for food in a ploughed paddock, and as the car went by they swept into the air on rose-hued wings. The unexpectedness of their wings bursting into that lovely flame color was so dramatic and effective that it was breathtaking.

Abby exclaimed in admiration, and Luke said, 'Galahs,' with the indifference of someone who had seen the sight many times.

But the strange flat empty landscape had been momentarily lit up and Abby stared after the birds until they were no more than black specks in the sky.

'That was a clever name to use for a lipstick,' she said. 'If it could be used with that much dramatic effect I should think the makers would make a fortune.'

'They probably hope to,' said Lola.

'They why don't they advertise? Instead of being so extraordinarily elusive.'

183

Lola shrugged. 'Perhaps they're not ready yet. The ones I had were only samples, you know.'

Abby turned in astonishment.

'Then why didn't you tell me, if you knew that? Here I've been making all sorts of enquiries.'

'I didn't know myself. You got me interested, after all this flap about a cosmetic company you couldn't find. I asked my boss.'

'Then didn't he know where the lipstick was made?'

'No. It had just been sent to him. You know, a publicity stunt. He said he threw away the literature.'

'But they called it Galah, a name to be remembered,' Abby said softly. And then, because they were a long way from all the things that had bothered and haunted her, she said impulsively, 'I've another angle to follow when we get back on Monday. It's becoming a thing with me to work this out, like solving a detective story.'

'What angle?' said Luke.

'Oh, just a voice on the telephone, a very tired voice of an old woman with arthritis.'

'Good heavens, Abby! You're getting as fanciful as Deirdre. Isn't she, Luke?'

Luke looked sideways at Abby. 'And much more devious,' he said. 'When did you do this, darling, and why didn't you tell me?'

'You wouldn't have believed me. Would

184

you?'

'And doesn't now, I should think,' said Lola.

'But they'll all tie up,' Abby said with certainty. 'The man who threatened me and called me the little lady in red, the burglar who didn't want my jewellery, that fat woman who sold me the toy swing, and now this, this old, tired voice. I'll find them all when I find that old woman.'

'And all this because of a harmless lipstick called Galah. Really, Abby!'

'Oh, I expect the lipstick is just a cover-up for something else. It must be.'

Luke said with some ruefulness, 'I think Abby must have been very bored, just with housekeeping and a husband? What do you think, Lola? If she sees all those sinister things in city life, what's she going to see in this prehistoric landscape and her first kangaroo?'

'And an emu or two,' added Lola. 'Really, Abby, you are a child. Wait till we tell Milton and Mary this.'

'I think not,' said Luke. His hand slid across and briefly, without Lola's awareness, pressed Abby's knee. It seemed to be a secret signal of love and protectiveness. He didn't want his silly little wife laughed at. 'We're here to enjoy ourselves. We've had enough of the lipstick theme. As a subject, let's make it taboo for this week-end.'

'Suits me,' said Lola. 'Are we going to get there before dark?'

'I doubt it. We've still a hundred miles to go.'

'When are we going to see a kangaroo?' asked Abby.

'Any time now. You've got to watch. They look like tree stumps in the distance in this sort of country.'

It was true that the country was primeval. The sun was sinking, and as the light died the vast, flat plain, grassless and waterless, turned to a monotonous gray and silver. Dead trees like bones stuck up at crazy angles, stunted gums turned black in the fading light. There was no sound but the purr of the car on the dusty road, and the constant harsh squawk of crows, like petulant babies.

Mary and Milton were ahead, their car lost in a cloud of dust.

'They can't have seen any roos or they'd have stopped,' Lola said. 'How disappointing. There ought to be some about.'

But there was nothing except the swooping crows, a tawny shape in the distance that was a fox eating a dead sheep, and suddenly three emus, ghost gray, moving bunchily away on their long legs. Luke stopped the car to watch them. Lola got out, stretching.

Then she exclaimed, 'Luke! Roos!'

And he was beside her, staring at the gray shapes, as still as the tree stumps, their heads turned to stare, their hands clasped loosely and meekly in front of them.

Luke got his gun and he and Lola began to move stealthily across the flat ground. A little later he fired, and the gray shapes leapt into the air and began to move away, with springy bounds. Luke and Lola followed until they were almost lost from sight, and Abby was alone in the car, alone in that great stillness. Even the crows had stopped squawking. There were no lights, no wind, nothing moving, just the growing dark, the great cloudless shining sky, and silence.

Suddenly she was overcome with the uncanniness. The landscape was too eerie, too indifferent to human life or life of any sort. Parched, colorless, unchanged for a billion years. And she was here alone.

That was it. She had been alone ever since she had come to Australia. For Luke's spasmodic displays of passion and strange remorse comforted her only temporarily. Now she was alone again, the odd one out, the stranger, the person who had uncomfortable fancies and premonitions, like Deirdre who thought she might be killed . . .

For even here, in this vast empty plain, she had the oddest sensation that she was being watched.

She scrambled out of the car, and stood shivering and calling, 'Luke! Luke, come back!'

And all at once, out of the dusk, from behind a clump of prickly bushes, he and Lola appeared, walking unhurriedly and talking.

They couldn't understand Abby's upset.

'I was frightened,' she said defiantly. 'I don't care if you do think I'm a baby.'

'You're a baby all right,' said Lola kindly. 'Silly little thing.'

But Luke was more serious.

'Why are you crying? Did something happen to frighten you? You can't cry just from sitting alone in the car!'

'I can,' said Abby. 'It's all so melancholy. Can't you see?'

But they didn't see anything except her foolish squeamishness. An English girl, not bred to the great spaces and an antiquity that wasn't man-made. They despised her a little. They couldn't possibly understand that this countryside was exactly the visual expression of all her strange fears and premonitions. It was a nightmare realized. But even Luke couldn't see that. They were all going to be sorry they had brought her, and Milton most of all. She dreaded facing Milton.

'Let's get on,' Luke said briefly. 'Abby's just overtired. I suppose this is a bit overwhelming, seeing it for the first time, and at dusk. It will be better tomorrow when the sun's shining.'

(But sunlight would emphasize the stark bones of the dead trees and the prickly shrubs and the bare red earth . . .)

'Though I'm afraid the pub we're going to isn't going to cheer you up much. This is the outback. I warned you. You really shouldn't have come.'

'All she needs is a sizeable neat brandy,' said Lola. 'But if you're going to be as scared as this, Abby, you'd better stay behind when we go shooting tomorrow.'

* * *

Mary and Milton were settled in when they arrived at the single-storey, wooden hotel in the little, one-street town. They were both at the bar, Milton in his chair, and seemed to be in conversation with several of the local inhabitants.

'There you are at last,' said Milton. He smiled at Abby, 'You look pretty tired. Come and have a drink.'

'We stopped to have a shot at some roos,' explained Lola. 'We all need a drink.'

The other men had turned to stare, in the uninhibited way of people who didn't see many strangers. One in particular, a brawny looking person with a shock of dark hair, seemed anxious to be friendly.

'You folks haven't had the journey I've had. Overland from Darwin. It's some pull.'

'What are you doing up this way?' asked Luke.

'Just looking round. I might push on to Sydney, or I might make for the Barrier Reef. Name's Mike Johnson. This your wife?'

189

He was looking at Lola. With her sun-burnt face and breezy air it was a forgiveable mistake. She looked like Luke's partner. But Luke's hand was round Abby's, impatiently or possessively, she wasn't sure which.

'No, this is my wife. And she needs a drink. We've had a long day.'

'Frankly, this country scares me stiff,' Abby said.

Everybody laughed. They recognised her English voice, and were tolerant. Even Milton said, 'I agree with you, Abby. It is frightening. Those great spaces. Life and death mean nothing. Time means nothing.' He hitched himself in his chair. 'Perhaps that's why I like coming here. A perspective on life is a good thing.'

But did he understand her strange eerie fear? She didn't think so.

'You don't look tired at all,' she said.

'Oh, I can travel. That's one thing I can do. But Mary's had it. She's had to do all the driving. You three girls had better all have an early night.'

Mary nodded. 'I'm all for that. You, too, Abby? I warn you, the rooms aren't the height of comfort. But I'm tired enough not to care.'

'Me, too,' said Abby cheerfully. 'I'll sleep like a log.'

*　　　*　　　*

She really thought that she would, too, when she was ready for bed. She had had a bath in the primitive bathroom where, though the water ran pale amber with rust, at least it was hot, and put on her warm dressing-gown. Luke had been right in warning her that the nights here were cold. The late spring frosts were sharp, and the walls and roof of this ramshackle hotel very thin.

Mary and Milton had the double room on one side of Abby's and Luke's, and Lola was on the other side. Across the linoleum-covered passage were three other rooms, one of them no doubt occupied by the black-haired man from Darwin. Abby hoped the late-comers to bed would not be too noisy. Every sound was audible, including the voices and laughter from the bar.

Dinner had been a rather poor meal, tough mutton washed down, on Milton's insistence, with plenty of tart, red Australian burgundy, and then rice pudding. The service, performed by a middle-aged woman with crimped, blonde hair, was casual and friendly.

'I warned you the meat was tough,' she said. 'You'd better have some more wine.'

'Bring another bottle,' said Milton. Milton either didn't mind roughing it, or was mellowed by the change from what must be the deadly boredom of his life. He was affable and amusing, and succeeded even in rousing Mary to animation.

The wine was brought by another woman with a pale, cadaverous face, like a drawing by Charles Addams. After the drinks they had already had at the bar, it succeeded in making Abby pleasantly relaxed and sleepy. She and Mary were very willing to have an early night, but Lola showed no intention of leaving the men. She seemed to be finding the man from Darwin stimulating company, which was a welcome change from having her eyes constantly on Luke.

As Abby was fixing her face in front of the spotty mirror, Luke looked in.

'You all right?' he asked.

'Fine. Sleepy.'

'Then have a good rest. I won't be late.'

'Are you going back drinking?'

'For a while. The boys expect it in a place like this.'

He came over to kiss her. But he wasn't thinking of her. There was an odd brightness in his eyes, a suppressed excitement. He was obviously stimulated, not depressed, by the overwhelming landscape. He was an Australian. Perhaps that explained it. Or perhaps he had just had a little too much to drink.

'Hope the bed's more comfortable than it looks,' he said.

'I don't suppose it is. The blankets are threadbare.'

'Keep your dressing-gown on.' He was at

192

the door, anxious to get back to the party. But he paused, 'You're not scared now, are you?'

'No. I'm sorry for that exhibition. But I really was scared.' The eeriness of the remembered scene came to her, and a faint shiver went over her.

'I must be crazy,' she said.

'Perhaps not as crazy as you think,' he said, and the door closed after him.

So perhaps he had caught a fragment of her feelings and understood. Abby accepted the slender comfort. Luke's footsteps died away, merging into the general noise coming from the bar. A little later there were other footsteps along the passage, and soon afterwards someone was whistling softly a very familiar tune. *But I love only you-oo, I love only you . . .*

Jock's tune! Abby sat upright in bed. Surely Jock wasn't here! She caught back her alarm and excitement, remembering that this was a hit tune, and that plenty of people liked it, even as obsessionally as Jock did. All the same, she got out of bed, and tiptoed to the door, to take a surreptitious look outside.

At that precise moment Mary's door opened and she did the same thing. Abby began to giggle.

'Did you hear it, too?'

'Hear what?'

'That tune. The one Jock plays all day. Someone's just been whistling it.'

'Oh,' said Mary. She wasn't particularly interested. But she was fully dressed, Abby saw, and looked cold, her arms folded tightly across her chest. 'I thought I heard Milton coming. Do you mean to say, Abby, you got up to see who was whistling that silly tune? You're an awfully nervous person, aren't you? I thought I was bad enough. Milton keeps me on edge, although he doesn't mean to, poor darling. But you jump at your own shadow. Have you always been like that?'

Now that Mary was giving her the attention she usually reserved for Milton, Abby was on the verge of trying to describe the small private fog of bewilderment she walked about in, so that everything seemed distorted, even an innocent tune being whistled. But why bother poor Mary with her problems? She had enough of her own.

'I'm all right. I'm just not acclimatised. And I guess I'm tired. You look tired, too. I thought you were going to bed early.'

'I have been resting. But I can't undress until Milton comes. He has to be helped. He can manage with his sticks a certain amount, but he can't get into bed.'

'It's wearing you out,' said Abby sympathetically.

Mary gave a long sigh.

'Yes. It's been hard on us both. But soon—' She paused, as if afraid to express her hope.

'You really think there's a chance he'll walk

194

again.'

'Oh, yes. A very good chance. It's his determination as much as anything.'

For a fleeting moment there was a look of Lola in Mary's face, a hard driving determination, that made her look quite different, a real person. Then it had gone, and Abby wondered if she had imagined it, for Mary merely looked pale and tired and subdued, accepting her troubles uncomplainingly.

'You'd better get some sleep, Abby. We've got that long drive to do all over again tomorrow. I'm used to it, but you're not. And don't listen to noises, or goodness knows what you'll hear in a place like this. We warned you it wasn't the Ritz.'

Shortly after Abby had gone back to bed she heard Lola's door slam, and then Lola's voice saying sharply, 'S-s-sh!'

So Lola was not alone in her room. Who was with her? The black-haired man from Darwin? Or the person who had whistled Jock's tune? Had it been a prearranged assignment, or just a pick-up?

Furious with herself for having heard anything at all, Abby buried her head in the pillow. But now sleep was impossible, for apart from the noise, and the hardness of the bed, she had got thoroughly chilled. If she were to sleep she would have to get a hot water bottle.

She switched on the light wearily. There was

no bell to ring. That was hardly to be expected. She would have to go and find a maid, or fill the bottle herself.

Tiptoeing to the door again, she stumbled clumsily against the wooden chair at the foot of the bed. Now she had probably startled everyone. But the only sound she heard was the click of Lola's door closing. She waited a moment then, not wanting to see who left Lola's room.

When it seemed safe, she stepped out into the passage, just in time to see a man, who had obviously lurked a moment himself, disappearing round the turn of the passage into the bar.

The electric light hanging from the ceiling had no shade. It made a bright, revealing light. But the man had moved quickly and Abby caught only a glimpse of him as he turned the corner. She could never have sworn that his sparse hair was the color of flesh. The bright light had merely dazzled her, and she had had too many fancies.

Someone was saying behind her, 'Do you want something?'

She turned to see the cadaverous woman who had brought them the wine at dinner. She looked as if she lived in a cellar herself.

'I wondered if I could have a hot water bottle.'

She was shivering violently. There was no need to explain that she was cold.

'Sure,' said the woman. 'Have you got your own bottle?'

Abby shook her head. It had been hot in Sydney, she wanted to say. The lizards came out in the warm afternoon sun.

'Then I can lend you one. I'll show you where you can fill it.'

The kitchen was a large, old-fashioned, country kitchen. A tabby cat with a very round head like an orange mewed and rubbed round her ankles. Abby waited restlessly for the kettle to boil. The bar was just across the passage from her. It had a colored glass door inset with narrow bands of clear glass. It was perfectly simple to go and peer through the glass and see if the fish-faced man was drinking with Milton and Luke. Like an old friend . . .

But contrary to her expectation there was no sign of him. Luke and the black-haired man from Darwin were sitting at the linoleum-covered table, and Milton had his chair drawn up close to them. Luke seemed to have been asked some question, for the other two men were waiting with what seemed deep interest for his answer.

Finally he nodded. He didn't speak. But his nod was all that was required, for both other men relaxed and smiled. Then Milton signalled the bar keeper for more drinks.

There were only three other men and a woman at the bar. None of them had sparse, flesh-colored hair.

The kettle was spitting and boiling furiously in the kitchen. Abby rescued it, and filled her bottle, slightly scalding one finger as her trembling hand slopped the water. The stubborn cat wanted to follow her back to her room. She shut the door on it, and went back down the passage, opening Lola's door as if absently.

'Oh, I'm sorry!' she exclaimed. 'I thought this was my room.

Lola was sitting on the side of the bed half undressed. She looked up from peeling off a stocking.

'Thought you'd have been asleep hours ago.'

'I was. But I woke frozen. I've just got a hot bottle. I don't know when on earth Luke is coming to bed.'

'Oh, men,' said Lola. 'This is their week-end off. You mustn't interfere. Wives are easily forgotten, I'm telling you. They can't compete with shooting, golf or a man's drinking. Something you'll have to learn, honey.'

There was nothing to show that she hadn't been alone in her room. Her face had its usual expression of careless friendliness. Though she seemed to have the same strung-up, bright-eyed look that Luke had had.

Abby couldn't say, 'Did you just have the fish-faced man in your room?' They were sick of her fancies—or what they called her fancies.

'When Luke comes to bed, you might let me have that hot bottle,' Lola was saying. 'I haven't got a man to keep me warm.'

From sheer tiredness, Abby had fallen asleep before Luke came to bed. She only half woke, and was unable to think where she was.

But when Luke bumped heavily into bed she roused herself.

'Have a nice evening, darling?'

His breath smelled strongly of brandy. He was a little drunk.

'Dammit, not the big fish!' He didn't seem to realise he was speaking aloud.

Abby's heart stopped. So he must have seen the fish-faced man, too.

'Then who is he?' she whispered.

But Luke was asleep.

CHAPTER THIRTEEN

In the gray light of early morning Abby thought critically that she was too self-disciplined. Last night she should have screamed and shouted and demanded that this wretched hovel of a hotel be searched to make sure that the fish-faced man, that surreptitious lurker, had not been in Lola's room.

But even if found, of what could she accuse him? He wouldn't admit to that empty room in Kings Cross, to his threats, to even having seen her before. She would be met with blank stares of bewilderment, and the watch on her would be increased.

Was it better to say nothing, to be apparently unaware of his presence, and of his intrigue with Lola, at least? To be forewarned was to be forearmed . . .

But what was it all about? Her reason was ruling her too much. Making a fuss, she might have found out more.

She nudged Luke awake.

'M-mm,' he muttered. 'What's the matter?'

'Luke, who's the big fish you were talking about last night?'

'Big fish? Haven't a clue.' He was fast asleep again.

'Wake up, Luke! I've got to know. It's time you told me something. Unless you're my

200

enemy, too.'

She was whispering urgently, remembering the thin walls.

Luke came awake reluctantly and bad-temperedly.

'What the devil are you talking about?'

'You said you hadn't got the big fish last night. Remember?'

His eyes, tired and old, looked at the ceiling.

'I must have been drunk.'

It was funny, thought Abby, there they were lying in bed together, two happily married people. Presently they would be brought tea by the blonde housemaid, or the cadaverous woman, would get up and wash and dress and go through all the motions of living in a polite and civilized fashion together. But their minds, guarded and secret, might have been a million miles apart.

She was just as alone in that moment as she had been in the bleak landscape last night.

Then Luke woke more completely and seemed to realize he had been rude. Or indiscreet.

'Sorry, sweetie. What was I saying? Or what were you saying? God, what a dump this is! Why doesn't someone bring us some tea?'

'Is anyone staying here besides us?' Abby asked.

'Only that chap from Darwin, and a couple of commercial travellers, I believe. They're all on their way to Brisbane today.'

Small as the town was, this wasn't the only hotel. Ramshackle hotels and bars were a feature of the outback. It wasn't much use asking questions because if the fish-faced man were shrewd (and there would be no doubt of that), he wouldn't stay under her very nose.

'By the way, that chap Johnson put me on to a good job in Darwin,' Luke said casually.

'Darwin! Will you go?'

'I don't know. I'll see what happens.'

I hate Australia, thought Abby. This mucky room with fluff under the dressing-table, this horrible bed. And Luke had said the week-end was to do them good!

Luke was leaning over her, watching her.

'Cheer up, honey. I mightn't need to do that job. I hope I won't have to.'

*　　*　　*

In contrast to her own queer unexplainable feeling of dread about the day ahead of them, and Luke's private worry, carefully hidden now that he was fully awake, the others were intolerably cheerful.

Milton, looking wonderfully fit and refreshed, was anxious to make an early start. Abby wondered how someone crippled as he was could have got adequate rest in the sort of beds this hotel provided. But Mary said that that was one thing Milton could still do, sleep anywhere.

202

'But you look as if you didn't sleep much, Abby.'

'Not much,' Abby admitted. 'It was too cold and too noisy. I could hear everything through those thin walls.'

She looked directly at Lola, and Lola's bright mocking eyes stared back.

'I slept,' said Lola. 'Cold and noise and all.'

'Come along, you girls,' called Milton briskly. 'We want to get off. We're taking a picnic lunch, Abby. We'll show you how we boil the billy out here. It's going to be a good day.'

It was, too. The sky, a pure shining blue, lifted its tremendous arch over the little town, flat and ramshackle and infinitesimal in this vast land. The air was crisp and chilly, but promised warmth. A bustle went on as Luke and their black-haired friend from the previous evening carried out luggage and stowed it in the cars. Milton watched with interest.

'No more in my boot,' he said. 'It's full. Well, let's get started. Come along, Mary.'

'Yes, darling. Coming.'

Presently they were off. The cadaverous woman and a thin sheepdog watched them go. There was no sign of the fish-faced man. But there were several cars parked along the street. Which one was his, and when would he begin to follow?

The endless road stretched ahead. There

was no car but Mary's and Milton's in front, and none behind.

Abby began to think her fears preposterous.

In spite of the lack of sport—during the morning only a few kangaroos a long way off were sighted—everyone remained cheerful. At mid-day they stopped for lunch. Milton wheeled his chair out and sat in the brilliant sunshine while the girls gathered sticks and Luke lit a fire, balancing the smoke-blackened billy over it.

It was relaxing and peaceful. The landscape was no longer sinister, but immensely calm and forgotten, as if even nature had discarded it, except for the stunted gums and thorny bushes. The crows rose and fell against the blue sky, crying harshly. The dead gum leaves crackled beneath Abby's feet. She was warm and well-fed, and inclined to agree with Milton that this escape from the city was to be cherished.

Milton leaned back in his chair, his strange eyes gleaming through narrowed lids.

'Well, Abby. Does this impress you?'

'Immensely.'

She thought she liked Milton a little better today. His anger was less apparent. He hadn't made a single scathing remark to his wife. He was living in a small bubble of contentment, obviously putting thoughts of the coming week out of his mind.

'Are you glad we brought you?'

Abby smiled serenely.

'I was coming, anyway. Wasn't I, Luke?'

'I guess you were, if you'd made up your mind. I have a stubborn woman for a wife.'

Even Luke was speaking with lazy tolerance.

'Stubbornness can be dangerous,' said Milton. He yawned and Mary began fussing.

'Are you tired? Why don't you take a nap? There's no hurry to move, is there?'

'Don't fuss, Mary. I'll get enough of that in the hospital next week.'

'How long is this session to be?' Luke asked.

'I don't know. Two or three weeks, probably. But this time I'll come out on my own two legs. I promise you.' There was a look of suppressed excitement and determination in his face. He waved his arm round the landscape. 'The next time I'm out here if I see old man roo across that piece of scrubland I'll go after him on my feet.'

'Of course you will,' said Mary.

'Don't humor me!' Milton's familiar irritation flashed out. 'You don't believe a word of it, but I'll show you. My God, I'll show you!'

'Not now, Milt,' murmured Lola. 'It's too exhausting. I'm going to take a nap, if you're not.'

'I'm going for a walk,' said Abby, standing up. 'Nobody needs to come with me.' She didn't look at Luke. 'I just want to explore. Am I likely to find any animals?'

'Probably only lizards,' said Milton. 'Give us a shout if you see any roos. Luke, Mary was having a little trouble with starting the car further back. I wish you'd have a look at it.'

'Okay,' said Luke. 'Don't go too far, Abby.'

Abby walked quickly over the dry earth, waiting for her anger with Milton to leave her. He had deliberately stopped Luke from coming with her. But if Luke had wanted to come, he could have said he'd look at the car later. What was this hold the Moffatts had over him? She was completely losing patience with them and their private dramas. Except for Deirdre, poor little wretch. The time was coming jolly soon when she would tell Luke he must choose between the Moffatts and her. Lola with her secret intrigue, Mary with as much spirit as a mouse, Milton a sick tyrant. What *did* Luke see in them?

But the blazing sunshine and the strange tormented landscape washed in yellow light soothed her, and her resentment began to dissolve. She walked on, all at once enjoying her loneliness and solitude. She had a desire to lose herself briefly in this impersonal plain, to get out of sight of the cars and people, and have a little time of utter relaxation.

The only sounds were lonely ones, the crackle of the gum leaves in a sudden breeze, the constant harsh cry of the crows, sheep calling intermittently far in the distance. Once she thought she heard her own name called,

206

'Abby! Abby!' but when she looked back she found she was out of sight of the cars. They must have been down that slight hollow behind the dried creek. How odd! She thought she would have been able to see them clearly from a long distance. But there was nothing except a faint puff of dust in the distance.

She stood still, pondering. In spite of the hot sunshine, she shivered faintly. Something of the eeriness of the previous night touched her again. She turned to go back, and at that moment the rifle shot cracked through the stillness.

Instinctively Abby fell flat. She hadn't been hit. For a moment she thought she had been. She did know that the bullet had come perilously close. The dust had whipped up at her side.

She was almost certain, as she lay rigid, that there had been no kangaroos in sight.

The shot must have been meant for her.

It was a long time before she could bring herself to move. There were no more shots, but suddenly, from a group of gum trees, the uncanny laughter of a flock of kookaburras began. It ran its gamut of harsh squawks and chuckles. It seemed that the whole countryside was laughing at her, lying in the dust, afraid to move.

When at last she stood up, scarcely daring to breathe, nothing at all happened. The kookaburras were silent, the landscape empty.

But not quite empty. Along the dusty ribbon of road, far away, was a car travelling very fast. It could have been anyone, a commercial traveller on his way to Sydney, a farmer on his way to some distant homestead.

Abby's paralysis of fear left her. She began to run, stumbling now and then, towards the hollow where the cars were.

When she reached the place they had gone. There was only the dead fire still emitting a thin wisp of smoke.

The long, straight road stretched into infinity. Far away there was a clump of tall gums and a high water tower which suggested a homestead. In complete panic Abby wondered if she must make her way there, all the time stalked by an unknown assailant with a gun.

But was he someone she would recognise all too well if they came face to face?

Where were Luke and Milton, Lola and Mary, all of whom carried guns? Why had they gone and left her? Was this something they had concocted late last night over their drinks in the bar? They knew, or at least Lola and Luke knew, how frightened she had been when alone for only a few minutes in the darkening landscape the previous evening. So how could Luke, her husband, who said he loved her, go and leave her?

Abby could no longer think coherently. She only knew that all her premonitions last night about this uncanny and hostile land had turned into this gigantic nightmare. Even in broad daylight the horrible stark eeriness had come back.

What was she to do? Stand forlornly on the roadside waiting for a passing car? And who would be in the car? Another enemy?

Everyone she encountered seemed to be an enemy, the fish-faced man, old Jock lurking suspiciously, the cosy woman with the too bright eyes, even the dressmaker, Miss Court, of the far-off ghostly voice ...

And now the Moffatts and Luke, deliberately deserting her ... There had been nothing wrong with the engine of Mary's car. It had been an excuse to keep Luke. Or perhaps an excuse Luke sought ... Suddenly Abby was remembering her slip on the cliffs above the Gap, Luke's grip on her arm, and then his intense distress. But had it been distress—or remorse for something he had planned and not quite achieved?

The cloud of dust in the distance was visible before the car itself. It was travelling at high speed. Abby had a momentary desire to run for cover. She pulled herself together sharply. For since whoever was in this car was coming miles from the opposite direction he could not have been her assailant.

She had to stop the car, from sheer self-preservation. She stood boldly on the roadside and when the car pulled up with a squeal of brakes and she saw Luke at the wheel, her first feeling was one of intense joy and relief.

It didn't matter in that moment that he might be her enemy. The joy was instinctive and automatic.

It had to be replaced by caution. As Luke opened the door and sprang out the other horrible feeling of suspicion nagged at Abby again.

He was looking so unconcerned, as if nothing had happened. Too unconcerned . . .

'Sorry we left you, darling. Lola spotted some kangaroos and we followed them for a few miles. But we lost them eventually. Didn't you hear me call you?'

'I was too far away.'

'Yes, that was the trouble. We'd have lost the roos if we'd waited. Hey, what's the matter? You look scared stiff. Don't say you're nervous of the wide open spaces even in broad daylight.'

Abby heard the incredulity that was almost contempt in his voice. There was a cold knot of misery inside her.

'Wouldn't you be scared stiff if someone had just tried to kill you?'

'Kill you! Abby! This isn't true!'

She should have been glad that at least he wasn't laughing at her. Instead, the shock in his voice showed that he could believe it was true. This seemed to be the worst of all.

'The shot came close enough,' she said

stiffly. 'It happened over there. From that clump of bushes. Just afterwards the kookaburras made a fuss, as if they'd been disturbed.'

'Must have been someone taking a shot at a rabbit.'

'Do I look like a rabbit?'

He searched her face. The old tormented look was in his eyes. He wasn't trying to hide it any more.

'Abby, do you swear this is true?'

She held out her hands, palms up, showing the marks of dust.

'I lay flat on the ground for ages. I thought then that whoever it was might think I was dead and go away.'

Luke didn't speak for a long time. Then he said slowly, 'This couldn't have happened. Never!'

She had never seen his face so stern, so old. She could hardly bear it. She wished that he hadn't believed her. She knew now that in all the panic and fright she had scarcely believed it herself. No one could really want to kill her!

'Perhaps it wasn't really me he was shooting at,' she said quickly. 'You've always said I jump to conclusions. Perhaps there was a rabbit, or even a kangaroo. The country seemed big enough to walk in safely. Then what should we do? Try to find this man? Although he's probably fifty miles away by now. I saw a car travelling very fast.'

'The explanation would be too slick,' said Luke oddly.

'You mean there isn't even any point in finding out who it was.'

'I don't think there'll be any mystery about that.'

Abby knew that this time she wasn't jumping to a conclusion, she had logically reached one.

'The fish-faced man!' she breathed. 'Then if you knew all the time that he was dangerous why didn't you warn me? I thought I saw him at the hotel last night,' she added, and knew that this time Luke wouldn't laugh at her.

'Then for heaven's sake, why didn't you tell me?'

'I wasn't sure, and I didn't think you'd believe me. You've never believed anything else I've told you.'

'Abby!'

She backed sharply away from him.

'Don't touch me!'

His hands fell to his sides.

'Abby, you don't think I—' His face was stiff with shock.

'Then why have you been so odd, so secretive? What *can* I think?' The anger that flamed in her was welcome because it temporarily buried her fear. 'I've got sick of it, Luke. You might habitually think girls are pretty dumb, but I'm not that dumb. Was I your wife or a tame puppy to run after the

Moffatts? You came home at nights, shut in yourself, never telling me anything. You'd talk to Lola, but not to me. I expect you told her your plans, as you probably always have. It was I who was the intruder whom you'd had to be gentlemanly enough to marry. But if you behave like this, deceiving me, putting me in danger, why ever did you think you had to do a little thing like keep a promise to a girl to marry her?'

Luke took her arm roughly.

'Get in the car and shut up. We're getting out of here as fast as we can. If there's anyone prowling over there with a gun he'll be brought to an accounting, I can promise you. And if you can bear it, if you don't think that I might have murderous designs on you, we're driving back to Sydney alone. Lola can go with the others. We can finish our quarrel if you insist on it on the way.'

As she got in the car he went on, 'I've been unforgiveably and abysmally stupid. You don't know how a man gets when he follows an obsession. He sees straight ahead and not round any corner. I've been missing all the corners. But I do love you, Abby. If I'd had the faintest suspicion that anything like this could have happened to you, I'd never have let you leave England, much less let you do anything as crazy as marrying me. For God's sake, don't you believe me?'

'Then stop treating me like a Victorian

213

wife!' Abby exclaimed furiously. 'Trust me. Tell me what it is that you're up to. Tell me, if you can, why Lola has this spell on you.'

'Lola!' he said, in a tone of acute distaste. Then abruptly he put his hand over hers, looking into the distance. 'See the dust. They're coming back to see what's happened.'

'To find my body!' Abby whispered.

The stony look had left Luke's face. It was alive with fury and urgency.

'Listen, Abby. Can you behave as if nothing has happened until we get back to Sydney? This is rather important. I'll explain on the way, if we can get rid of Lola. There isn't time now. Can you?'

Abby shivered. 'I'm not anxious to try convincing Milton that anything has happened. He only listens to himself and his own tragedy.'

'Milton listens to everything, believe me. But can you trust me, Abby?'

The car approaching them was rapidly growing nearer. Abby wanted badly to say 'Yes' whole-heartedly. She remembered almost the same words on their wedding night, Luke saying desperately, 'Try to understand.' The words had had nothing to do with the act of love, after all. She might have known they hadn't. Luke had expected her to match him in passion. He hadn't thought he was making love to a scared mouse of a girl. The words had meant that she was to understand his subsequent strange behaviour.

But if he could let events take place that even led to the point of her life being in danger, it must have been for some desperately important reason.

'Tell me why I should trust you?'

'You remember Andrew?'

'Your brother? Of course. How couldn't I? Is he in this, too?'

'He was. He's dead.'

Abby's lips went dry.

'Oh, Luke! When? You never told me.'

'He died a few months ago. Actually, he was murdered and his body dumped in the Sydney harbor. There's no time to tell you more now.'

He was looking towards the rapidly approaching car. He had got a grip on himself and was hiding his fury. His profile was hard and austere. Abby knew the look that would be in his eyes, cold, withdrawn, much too old.

'I can go on acting, Luke,' she said quickly. 'You'll see.

The car came alongside and Lola sprang out. Abby was intensely aware of three pairs of eyes on her, but she didn't want to jump to any more conclusions. She couldn't decide whether the eyes held surprise or disappointment, or no particular emotion at all. She was not the only one with the ability to put on an act.

'Hi,' she said. 'Sorry you had to come back for me. I walked too far. Luke says you didn't get any roos, after all.'

'The beggers jumped in the wrong direction,' Milton said. His voice was as usual, flat, without pleasure.

'All that dash for nothing,' said Lola. She looked at Abby. 'I hope you weren't scared when you found we'd gone?'

'Scared!' said Abby. 'In broad daylight! Whatever could happen to me?'

'You didn't care much for it last night.'

'That was different. It was dark and uncanny. But if I could go for a walk alone, I wasn't scared, was I? Luke knew that.'

Luke put his head out.

'It's getting late, Milton. Time we were making for home. Abby and I will lead the way this time.' He started the engine and released the gears.

'Hey, wait for me!' said Lola.

Luke grinned. 'Thought you might like to ride with Mary and Milton. I want to show Abby some of the views from the Blue Mountains. It'll bore you.'

Milton had opened the door of his car. His face looked pale and bad-tempered.

'Sorry, Luke, there isn't really room in here for a third. My back's aching like the devil. I've got to stretch out.'

'Anyway,' said Lola, smiling, her golden eyes looking directly at Luke, 'I intend to sleep. You two lovebirds can prattle as much as you like.'

She got in without further invitation. Milton

216

called, 'Don't lose us, Luke. I'm still not too happy about the way this engine's behaving.'

'Then you'd better lead after all,' said Luke. 'I'll tail you. Abby and I can do the Blue Mountain trip another time. Sorry, darling.'

Abby knew that he was apologizing for having to keep her in the dark for a few more hours. She couldn't look at him, acknowledging her understanding, for Lola in the back would be watching them ceaselessly in the driving-mirror.

Now Lola added her careless apology. 'Sorry, kids. But Milt's in such a temper I couldn't stick three hundred miles of it. Poor Mary. But after all, she is his wife, and it's her job. Abby, you look worn out. Doesn't she, Luke? The color of paper. You must have walked too far. Or did you run into a dinosaur?'

'It wouldn't have surprised me if I had,' Abby answered lightly. 'I'm becoming fascinated with this country. I believe I'll even become an addict.'

More double talk. It was to comfort Luke and assure him that now she was all right. But Lola had interpreted her words in some other way.

'Addict? In what way do you mean?' Her voice was sharp.

'Not as applied to alcohol or drugs,' Luke explained. 'Abby means Australia can become an acquired taste to the newcomer. You're being a bit dim, aren't you, Lola?'

'And you sound revoltingly professorish,' Lola said tartly.

They made a little more desultory conversation, but now Abby didn't hear it. One of Luke's words had made a small signal in her mind. Addiction—as for drugs. The over-bright eyes of the plump woman in the toy shop, the everlasting keyed-up chatter of Mrs. Moffatt, the convenient forgetfulness and vagueness of the jeweller in the Cross who saw nothing and heard nothing . . .

These three people, at least, seemed to be under a spell. Who else? Perhaps Mary, so constantly meek and long-suffering. Not Lola, not Milton, with their sharp alert intelligence. But old Jock, lingering about persistently, the fish-faced man who would obey his terrible orders . . .

One thing only was starkly clear, and that was Luke's reaction to the news of the death of the unknown Chinese by drowning in the harbor. It had a connection with Andrew's death. For later that night, she remembered, they had talked of Andrew, lightly and lovingly, and Luke had hidden his grief for his brother whom he had so respected and loved. Poor, brave, clumsy, loving Luke whom now she trusted completely . . .

CHAPTER FOURTEEN

Deirdre had been in her bedroom but not in bed for a long time before she heard the cars come home. She jumped up from the floor where she had been sprawling in a bored fashion over a comic, and looked out of the window.

She was careful not to be seen because Gran had tucked her in hours ago, and would be furious. And then Mummy would be furious and there would be one of those boring rows.

She only wanted to see if Abby had come home safely. It had been an awful week-end, with Gran muttering and mumbling more than usual, and sad without Abby. There was no fun at all in looking through the windows of an empty house. She had even had to resort to an unsatisfactory conversation with old Jock who had been prowling about quite a lot. He said he'd been told to water the geraniums and keep an eye on the place, but Deirdre didn't believe a word of that. He was a prowler, like her.

Could it be he who walked in the house at night?

Luke had driven his car down and then come back to help take things out of Uncle Milton's car. Deirdre wondered if they might have brought back a kangaroo, and forgetting caution craned out to see. She watched disappointedly as they took nothing out of the boot but bags, and then several flat packages. No kangaroo. But Uncle Milton was in his usual bad temper.

When Luke had gone he wheeled himself into the house, and Deirdre heard acrimonious voices from the hall. It was, of course, Mummy quarrelling with him again. Mary didn't say a word. She never did.

But now Uncle Milton's voice rose angrily. 'He's a clumsy fool! Wait till I see him!'

'He is not. He's stood by you all all the time. My God, if it hadn't been for Reg—'

Deirdre's fingers flew to her ears. They were talking about the man who might be her father. She didn't want to hear what they were saying about him. She stood still for a long time, then, when she cautiously removed her fingers, the voices were quieter, even Uncle Milton's.

'Leave it now. I want a drink. Where's the kid?'

'In bed. Hours ago,' said Gran.

'Thank God for that.'

Deirdre's face sharpened with hatred. One day, she thought, one day she'd tip that old chair over when Uncle Milton was in it. Or let it run down the slope to the river. For God's sake, if Reg was her father, why didn't he come and rescue her?

Dejectedly she got into bed and settled down to sleep. But if she heard those footsteps tonight she would at last have the courage to go and see whose they were. She really would.

When the time came, however, she lay curled up and trembling. It must be very late, almost morning. She could see the moon tangled in the tall gums on the other side of the river. The footsteps were not loud. It was just that some part of her never quite stopped listening for them so that, measured and muffled as they were, she always woke.

After a long time she forced herself to get out of bed and tiptoe to the door. There she stood in her pyjamas shivering violently.

One, two, three, four, five, six, and then back, one, two, three, four, five, six. Long deliberate strides up and down the mosaic flooring of the hall.

Was it her father down there? Did he know he had an unhappy daughter upstairs? He couldn't, or he would have wanted to see her, months, years ago. He would have come to her birthday party. No one could ever have told him about her. He'd be quite surprised to see her. He would probably swing her up in his arms and say, 'You're not pretty—' (because she wasn't), 'but you're cute and I love you.'

But to have that happen he had to know about her. There was only one way to tell him, and that was to open her door and go to the head of the stairs and look down and say, 'Hi,

Daddy!'

It was crazy to be so scared. She wasn't scared of anything, really, not even those secret footsteps.

Deirdre's chin went up, and her hand softly turned the door knob. She opened the door noiselessly and saw the shaft of light across the stairs from the hall. Her pyjama trousers were slipping down. She had to tug fiercely at them, and in doing so got her foot caught in the hem of one drooping leg. She tripped, making a small thud. It wasn't a loud noise, but sufficient to halt the footsteps.

Petrified, she stood absolutely silent. Now the footsteps had started again, but briskly this time, and up the stairs.

A light flashed on. A figure, immensely tall, stood over her.

At last Deirdre dragged her eyes up and looked into the face that stared down at her. In that moment all her toughness left her. She gave a small whimper. Her face was stiff with fright.

CHAPTER FIFTEEN

Luke wouldn't let Abby out of his sight. He switched on all the lights, and drew the curtains, going from room to room with such meticulous care that at last Abby giggled.

'Darling, you're like a spinster looking for a man under the bed.'

'It's no laughing matter. We're not staying here. Pack the few things you need for the next day or so. We're going to a hotel.'

Abby sat down.

'I'm not moving from here until I know what this is all about.'

'I'll tell you what it's about. Tomorrow this house goes up for sale. Tonight we move and then get in touch with the police.'

He went to draw back the curtain slightly and look down to the river. A glow-worm light came from Jock's boat, and the usual tune, though muted, drifted up.

'At least Jock hasn't changed his habits,' said Abby with something almost like affection. 'I believe I'd miss him if we moved.'

'Not if, when. I hate this place as much as you do.'

Abby looked up, astonished. 'Luke! I haven't known a thing that's been going on in your mind.'

'I'm glad you haven't.' He came up to her,

223

holding out his hands. 'Smell my fingers.'

The faintly pungent odor was distinctive and clinging.

'What is it?' Abby asked.

'Opium. I've just been unloading it from Milton's car. That's what we went on this week-end for.'

'The man from Darwin!' Abby exclaimed. 'He was to meet you.'

Luke nodded. 'He's one of the syndicate. I hoped he would be the big boss, but he wasn't. He's a steward on one of the big airliners and has smuggled several supplies of the stuff. But like all of us, he's never actually met the boss. Got his orders by telephone in Singapore. This syndicate has been bringing in the opium for some time, and breaking it down to market it in other forms, heroin and morphine. This makes small quantities that can be hidden in tiny containers.'

'Such as lipsticks,' Abby breathed.

'You're too bright, darling. It was bad luck that lipstick came your way. What you thought was innocent was pretty deadly. You just had to lift the lipstick out and underneath was the powder. That's the way the stuff's been distributed.'

'And prepared by the Rose Bay Cosmetic Company?'

'That's right. Among a few other perfectly innocent cosmetics. They'd been operating in a small way in that building in the Cross, but last week they got windy. The police were getting suspicious. So it had to be a midnight flit, more or less. You walked in at the end of it. You were probably very lucky not to have been killed there and then. I didn't realise that at the time. I do now—after today.'

Luke looked at her with his remorseful eyes.

'Can you forgive me? I'm not good at this kind of game. I thought you would be perfectly safe so long as you remained ignorant of what was going on. In fact, I was assured you would be, and I believed them. So I helped Lola organise the camouflage for the next day when you went back to that room. I hoped you'd be fooled for the time being.'

'Little you knew me!' Abby murmured.

'So it seems. I could have wrung your neck at one stage. You're far more clever than me, actually. I should have told you all about this business at the beginning, but they'd never have trusted me if you knew. I'd worked a long time trying to get their trust. They only finally decided to take me in on it this week-end.'

'Why did you want their trust?'

'Because six months ago Andrew died, on this case. A ship from Hong Kong was in port and he went on board to do a little investigating. He never came off it alive. His death was hushed up by the department. No one connected him with me.'

'The ship that came in again the other day—with the dead Chinese?'

225

'Yes. The captain's a shady character, but the police can't so far pin anything on him.'

Abby's eyes were full of understanding and sympathy.

'So you picked up where Andrew left off?'

'I persuaded the police to let me do a little private investigating. I knew Andrew had got on to the Moffatts, but they seemed to be just receivers. We wanted the brains of the organization, a brilliant and ruthless person whom we believed travelled backwards and forwards to Singapore and Hong Kong, organising shipments and keeping the team together. The Moffatts were lesser fry. This is the man we want and must get.'

'Lola's husband?' suggested Abby intuitively.

'Could be. But I doubt it. I think her husband's one of the lesser fry, too. Indeed, I rather think he might be your friend with the fish-face.'

'Of course!' Abby exclaimed. 'He was in her room last night. I heard him. Oh, poor Deirdre!'

Luke stared. 'What's Deirdre got to do with it?'

'If that's her father, after all the hopes she's cherished.'

'I don't know what you're talking about. If ever I saw a child who was less of an idealist—'

'Rubbish. You don't know her!'

Luke sat down beside her. 'Abby! Abby

226

darling, you're such an extraordinary—'

Abby pushed him away.

'Don't let's waste time now. Go on with this story. So the Rose Bay Company had to move. Where is it now?'

'Nowhere. They're lying low for a while. They've stored their equipment at the Moffatts'.'

'Then why on earth don't the police seize it?'

'Because they haven't been told it's there. I told you, I'm waiting to get the big fish.'

'Rose Bay himself?' said Abby.

'Rose Bay?'

'Or she could be a woman,' Abby murmured.

Luke stared at her.

'A woman! I wonder. You might be right.'

'That old woman I spoke to on the telephone yesterday while you thought I was trying on girdles,' Abby said eagerly.

She was rewarded by his chagrined astonishment.

'You've been one jump ahead of me all the time.'

'Not all the time. But we must go and see this old woman first thing in the morning. We must be quick.' She looked at him soberly. 'There isn't much time, is there?'

'No time at all. That's why we're moving out of this house tonight.'

'Oh, no, we're not,' said Abby.

'We must. Don't you realize how ruthless they are? Now they're suspicious of you you're in danger all the time. My God, Abby, Andrew's dead, but you're alive, and I intend to have you stay that way. I've been foolhardy enough.'

'How long did it take you to get them to trust you?' Abby asked calmly.

'Ever since I met them and started negotiating to buy this piece of land. I had to have some perfectly innocent reason for meeting them. I even had to build a house where I didn't want it. Luckily I had a girl I was going to marry, so that part of it was plausible. And they knew I needed money. I was beginning my profession, building a house and getting married.'

'But I came before you were ready, didn't I?'

Luke nodded. 'I wanted all this behind me. I was obsessed with the thought of avenging Andrew's death. He was the only person I loved, except you. But I couldn't stand the thought of you being mixed up in such nasty business. Indeed, you couldn't be, because if I told you anything at all, I was out. The Moffatts don't trust other women—except addicts, of course. They, poor creatures, are too deeply involved to do anything. So come now. Pack your bag.'

'Don't be a fool,' said Abby. 'You're going to see this through. We're both going to.' She smiled at him serenely. 'First thing in the morning we'll pay another call on Miss Court, dressmaker. Agree? And now we'd better go to bed, or someone will be thinking our light's on too late. They'll wonder what we're finding to talk about for so long. And, Luke—I'm sorry about Andrew.'

His face twisted. 'You're too damned clever!'

'Come to bed,' Abby said gently.

'You see too much and you feel too much, and I love you.' His face was buried in her hair. 'I love you.'

CHAPTER SIXTEEN

'Couldn't it be Milton?' said Abby questioningly, at breakfast the next morning.

'Impossible. He's a cripple. He's never out of his chair. But I grant you, he could have the brain.'

'You're sure this man is in Singapore?'

'Not all the time, but frequently. He runs this organization like a battle, visiting all the units. We have proof of that.'

'And your trip to Darwin would have been to collect the next lot coming by plane?'

'If I make it.'

'You'll still make it, if necessary,' said Abby. It was surprising how happy she felt this morning, in spite of the difficulties and likely dangers ahead. Now she was really married. Now she had the husband she had expected and wanted. She was very happy indeed.

She tried not to let her eyes linger too long on Luke's eased and well-loved face. She had to remain calm and intelligent.

'Deirdre hasn't been down this morning. That's not like her, to neglect looking us over.'

'I thought she annoyed you.'

'She does, too, but I've sort of got fond of her.' Abby went out on the patio to look for the kookaburras. They sat faithfully on the jacaranda tree, watching her. They looked fat and well-fed and bathed in the morning sun.

'They're really awfully cute,' she said. 'I'll miss them when we leave here. Even if they do laugh at me.'

She went on round the house to look at the geraniums she had planted, and Jock gave her a friendly wave from his boat.

'I watered them,' he shouted.

To her surprise she found herself waving back quite happily. Even old Jock, the parasite, had no terrors for her now. Then she thought of the fish-faced man, and wondered where he had spent the night. All the way home yesterday, especially after it was dark, she had thought a car had followed persistently a long way behind.

Perhaps he had slipped down to Jock's boat, late. In that case Luke might be right that she shouldn't linger outside.

But no one would shoot a woman in her own garden, in a busy suburb. An accident in the open countryside was another thing altogether.

No, they'd try another way next time.

For all her happiness, Abby shivered. She went rather quickly inside, forgetting Deirdre.

'When are you going to the office, Luke?'

'I'm not.'

'As far as the Moffatts are concerned, you are. You must leave at the usual time and take Lola. I'll be coming to do some shopping in the city. It's easier to travel in early with you than to go by ferry later. When we've dropped Lola we can start on our own affairs.'

'If this is a woman,' Luke said, 'that places a different angle on it altogether. Rose Bay. A pseudonym, of course. A good password for customers. I wonder. You may be right.'

When Lola didn't appear at her usual time Luke said they would call for her. He noticed that Abby was wearing her red suit and said she looked charming. Abby didn't explain that wearing it was all part of getting her courage back and lending normality to the day. What did it matter if it made her conspicuous?

She sat in the car while Luke got out and rang the Moffatts' doorbell.

After some time Mrs. Moffatt appeared, still in a long woollen, rather grubby dressing-gown. Her hair looked more frizzled than ever and her brown eyes moist and anxious. She fingered at her throat, missing her strings of beads.

'Lola's gone,' she said. 'She's taken Deirdre to school.'

'As early as this!' Abby exclaimed from the car.

'They had exams, or something. She was fretting about not being late. Deirdre, I mean. Lola said to tell you she'd get a bus this morning. Anyway, it's saved Mary a trip. What with getting Milton's things ready for hospital, she hasn't really got the time. You look pretty, Abby. Pretty and gay.'

There was an air of forlornness about the little figure in the soiled dressing-gown. But Abby wouldn't let herself be moved by it. She had another anxiety.

'Luke, Deirdre's never yet fretted about being late for school,' she said as they drove away. 'She's done everything possible to be late. And if I know her, she'd be even later on exam day.'

'You say you know her.'

'I do, too. She's a lot like I was as a child. Unpleasant and aggressive only because she's shut out.'

'If you were ever unpleasant and aggressive, I'll believe all the nice things you say about Deirdre.'

'Seriously, Luke. And why didn't Lola call out and tell you not to wait for her? Let's drive past the school and see if we can see them.'

Luke agreed, and drove over the hilltop, cruising slowly down the road past the school. There were the blowing gums sparkling in the morning light, the stream of hurrying cars, and the chatter of children on their way to school. A bus drew up and Abby put her hand on Luke's arm to stop the car. They waited while a gaggle of children clambered down. No Deirdre. No slim, well-groomed Lola on her way to work in a smart beauty salon.

'We've missed them,' said Luke. 'Anyway, it isn't important.'

'No. I expect it was Lola who rushed

Deirdre off early for some reason. Perhaps she just didn't want her coming down talking to me.'

But she was remembering uneasily Deirdre's histrionic words, 'This is when I'll be killed,' and finding it not so easy now to laugh at them.

She was also realising for the first time, and with shocking clarity, that by this time she herself should have been dead for nearly twenty-four hours. Her inquisitive eyes, her mouth, safely closed. She had come rudely awake from the happy dream in which she had been ever since she had discovered Luke's true state of mind. A sense of urgency filled her. This was the baffling scene, with the glinting trees and the hurrying traffic and the uncaring children which she had experienced the day she had waited for Deirdre. It had led nowhere and she knew it would lead nowhere again.

'Let's get on,' she said urgently. 'I think we should hurry. I've a feeling—'

'What?'

'I don't know. As if we must do something awfully quickly.'

'I'm with you.'

She couldn't get rid of her tension as they drove into the city, sweeping over the great bridge and then up the wide thoroughfare to Kings Cross. She noticed that the rubber plant had been moved from the blue balcony, and a rather tatty fern put in its place. But the canary was still there, and it was singing. The shrill cheerful voice helped to dispel the ghosts.

'Luke, if I'd had the sense to ask in any more shops than those two, someone would have knows the Rose Bay Cosmetic Company, or seen their sign.'

'Probably. We counted on you doing exactly what you did. It was a risk, but it had to be taken. We didn't think you'd go back there again. We all underestimated you.'

'Oh, I can be inquisitive, too. Tell me, had you met that woman in the toyshop before?'

'No, I hadn't. But I've only just been accepted in this organization. They don't encourage meetings.'

'Well, I'm sure it was she who rang and told me to go to Rose Bay. She must have had some feeling of remorse, or something.'

'We'll soon find out,' said Luke briefly.

They got out of the car and Luke took her arm.

'When we've settled this affair I'll bring you up here to enjoy the Cross.'

Abby sniffed the scent of carnations. She saw a fruit vendor behind his magnificently stocked barrier of fruit smiling at her. She remembered the astringent kindness of the woman in the house with the rubber plant and the canary.

'I've got friends up here already.'

The black lace dress was still in the window, which scarcely surprised Abby. It looked too tired to be worn. In the shop the stupid girl was dusting the counter. She looked up, her mouth dropping open.

'Oh, it's you again. If you want Miss Court—'

'We do.'

'She isn't in yet. She might not be in today. She's been all over the place lately, sometimes here, sometimes not.'

'Then what about her new assistant?' said Abby pleasantly. 'The rather stout woman who's just started work here.'

'Just started? Who do you mean? There's only me and Miss Court. I mind the shop and Miss Court sews at home and comes in later for fittings.'

Abby felt a swift urge of excitement.

'Then we'll have to see her in her home, Luke, won't we? We can't mess about like this any longer.' Her voice was firm and authoritative as she asked, 'What's her address?'

'I'm not supposed to give it, madam. Only to special clients.' The girl had begun to look serious, catching their tension.

'I think you could call us special clients,' said Luke, curtly. 'It will save us looking up the telephone book. What's the secrecy, anyway?'

'She doesn't like to be bothered at home. But if you insist—it's 14 Beachey Road, Darling Point. And I hope you'll explain you made me tell,' she called after them.

*　　*　　*

The house was one of a row of similar houses, shaped like a box and surrounded by a small and neglected garden. There were lace curtains at the windows. The place had something in common with the dresses Miss Court made, an uninspired and dispirited look.

Luke rang the bell, and it was only then that Abby wondered how they were going to open the conversation.

'We won't beat about the bush,' Luke said, reading her thoughts. 'We'll ask for Rose Bay. There's always a split second when a person shows reaction, even if she covers up immediately.'

After a long time, however, it was a very old woman who opened the door. She leaned on a stick. Her face was a mass of seamed wrinkles, the only surviving feature of any distinction the great pointed nose. Dim, washed blue eyes, half blind, peered at Luke and Abby. The petulant quavering voice that Abby remembered on the telephone said, 'You'll be looking for my daughter, I daresay. She's not in.'

'The person we're looking for,' said Luke clearly, 'is someone called Rose Bay. Can you help us?'

There was no split second reaction, no reaction at all.

'You're a long way out of your way.' The old knotted hand lifted the stick to wave vaguely in another direction. 'This is Darling Point. Rose Bay's miles away.'

'But it's a woman we're looking for, not a place.'

There was a faint reaction then, but only one of perplexity.

'There's no one called Rose Bay here. You've come to the wrong place. Sorry I can't help you. I'm no use to anybody now, you know. I have the arthritis so badly. My daughter—'

'When will your daughter be in?'

'I wouldn't know that. She never tells me anything. She just says not to interfere. Nobody wants old people. We might as well be dead.'

She made to shut the door. Luke held it open.

'You are Mrs. Court, aren't you? And your daughter is a dressmaker.'

Now suspicion flared dimly in the less faded eyes.

'How do you know that?'

'Only because my wife has been to the shop repeatedly, and never found Miss Court there. So can we come in and wait until your daughter returns? She isn't in the shop so she can't be far away.'

'I don't know what you're talking about. First you want this other woman, then you want my daughter.' A ghostly firmness came into her voice. 'What is your business?'

'I want to discuss getting some clothes made,' said Abby. 'That girl in the shop is no use at all.'

'Oh, well, then you'd better come in. My daughter shouldn't be long. I think she only went shopping. But she never tells me anything. She could just as well be gone for the day.'

The old creature limped slowly down the narrow hall and led them into a depressing sitting-room. With a great many sighs and exaggerated care she lowered herself into a basket chair and went on ruminating.

'It's not right to be kept in the dark like this. My daughter has been brought up to be a good girl, but now she has these secrets. Men come at night. Oh, yes, they do!' Her arrogant nose lifted and challenged Luke and Abby to believe her. 'I don't make that up. I hear the doorbell and voices. I'm not completely deaf and blind.'

Abby heard the controlled excitement in Luke's voice.

'Has Rose always been a good girl until lately, Mrs. Court?'

'Rose? Who are you talking about? My daughter's name is Maud.'

'Then she has a friend called Rose?'

'This Rose Bay you've got on your mind? I don't know who she is. Sounds like a fortune teller. I don't think Maud's silly enough to be going to a fortune teller at her age. Though she does have this craze for lipsticks and powders and things. You should see her drawer!' The old woman's eyes glinted craftily. 'She doesn't know I looked. She left it unlocked one day. Well, what else have I to do? Doesn't she know it's a sad business sitting alone day after day? Not even allowed to answer the telephone because I get messages wrong! Oh, the old aren't wanted, I'm telling you. We might as well be dead.' The old lady's chin sank on to her chest. She had gone from them into a melancholy dream.

But all at once she roused herself and peered into the distance.

'Yes, I remember now. Someone asked for that woman on the telephone. That Rose Bay.'

And as if on cue the front door opened and the stout woman from the toyshop who had sold Abby the child on a swing came briskly in.

She saw Abby and Luke and stopped dead. Her eyes darted from them to her mother. All at once her face didn't look plump, but thin and harried.

'Mother, have you been talking nonsense again? I hope you haven't been believing what she said.' Her quick eyes had darted back to Abby and Luke. 'She's senile, you know. Well, what can I do for you?'

She had recovered herself. But the hand holding the shopping basket was clenched until the knuckles showed white.

'We're looking for Rose Bay,' said Luke pleasantly. 'My wife said you telephoned and told her to see Rose Bay. But the message has left us mystified. So we've come to you!'

'But you're—' Too late the woman stopped. 'I thought it was only her—'

'And that I was one of you,' finished Luke. 'I was, to a point. But only to a point. Now the situation's urgent and dangerous. Yesterday someone tried to kill my wife.'

'Kill!' The woman's hands flew to her mouth. Her eyes momentarily showed horror.

'You thought she might be in some danger, didn't you,' Luke went on kindly. 'That's why you telephoned that message. So now you can help us further. If you're not Rose Bay yourself, who is she?'

The woman's face went blank.

'I haven't a clue. I don't know what you're talking about.'

'I think you do. I also think you're a nice person who's got herself into this mess through an unfortunate weakness. You're an addict, aren't you, Miss Court?'

'No, not!' the woman whispered.

'Let me see your arm.'

'No!'

'Then shall we take a look at your supply of lipsticks and cosmetics?'

'Drawers full,' muttered the old woman, tapping her stick. 'Ridiculous vanity at your age, Maud.'

'You felt worried about my wife,' went on Luke. 'You are a nice person fundamentally. I'm sure you'd never willingly be involved in murder.'

Maud Court's eyes were dragged back to Luke's.

'It isn't true! They wouldn't go that far.'

'You know they're ruthless.'

She nodded unwillingly.

'Who knows, you could be the next. If they find out you warned Abby.'

'I had to. I didn't trust that Reg.'

'The man upstairs?' said Abby swiftly. 'The man who threatened me.'

The woman nodded. 'He's bad. He'd do anything. I wanted to get out of it myself, but you see—' Unconsciously she rubbed her arm up and down. Her face had crumpled. 'I can't,' she said despairingly.

'There are cures,' said Luke, still in his kind voice. 'Don't give up. But tell us who Rose Bay is. If you don't, we'll find out some other way, but it might be too late for one of us. It's too late for my brother.'

Slow comprehension came to Maud Court's eyes. They filled with tears which ran down her cheeks. She sobbed helplessly.

'I've been so unhappy. I've hated it. Caught in a net—I can't tell you who Rose Bay is. I can only tell you the number I ring. They take messages. I'll write it down for you.'

With a violently shaking hand she wrote the number on the telephone pad, and handed it to Luke.

Luke said quietly, 'Thank you, Miss Court. There's no use telling you there won't be trouble, because there will. But I'll do my best to see you get off lightly.'

He gave her shoulder a reassuring squeeze. The old lady in the chair peered with sudden sharp interest.

'Come, Abby,' said Luke. 'We've done all we can here.'

*   *   *

Out in the car he said, 'It's the Moffatts' number. You knew it would be, didn't you?'

'So we've still only got the go-between,' said Abby disappointedly. 'Unless it's Mrs. Moffatt. She looks sly enough sometimes. Or Lola.'

'Neither of them has been away during the last six months. Nor has Mary, though it would be fastastic to think of Mary. Rose Bay has been abroad in that time. So where are we?'

'There's only Milton left,' said Abby reflectively. 'And he's a cripple. Without his chair he's helpless.' She was thinking of Deirdre's heartless prank, wheeling the chair away and leaving him marooned in the toilet. But Deirdre had said . . .

'Luke, what hospital does Milton go to?'

'I don't know. He's secretive about that.

Refuses to have visitors while he's there. Sour brute.'

'Luke, I've an idea. Persuade Milton to let you drive him to the hospital this afternoon instead of Mary.'

'Is that any use?'

'He won't let you, of course. But keep on insisting. Make him lose his temper.'

'Shouldn't be difficult. What are you getting at?'

'Deirdre said the chair was full of cushions. That was just after I saw Mary wheeling it down the road. As if,' her words came very slowly, 'as if I were meant to think Milton was in it, when he wasn't.'

She had gone white.

'Do you know, it's terribly important that we find Deirdre very quickly!'

CHAPTER SEVENTEEN

In spite of their haste, Luke stopped at his office to make some telephone calls. He said they were urgent and couldn't be made from a public call box. Abby had to contain her impatience, and make conversation with Miss Atkinson.

'How's your mother?' she asked automatically.

'Not too bad at all, thank you, Mrs. Fearon. We've just got a television and she loves it. One thing I must say for her, there's nothing wrong with her brain. She's as bright as someone half her age.'

Different from another mother and daughter, Abby thought. Maud Court hadn't adjusted herself so well to her lot. But her mother was senile. Among other reasons, that could be one that had caused her to take to drugs. Poor Maud, caught between her conscience and her overmastering desire . . .

'I believe you had a lovely week-end, Mrs. Fearon,' Miss Atkinson went on brightly. 'What did you think of the outback?'

'I think it's very impressive.'

'Impressive, yes. But how people living there survive!'

Abby repressed a wry laugh. Luke appeared, looking brisk and efficient.

'We're off now, Miss Atkinson. Try to keep everyone happy. I'll be back to normal tomorrow. Abby and I have urgent things to do today.'

Miss Atkinson looked put-out and peevish as they hurried off. She returned to her typewriter with bored indifference.

'In spite of the excitement,' Abby murmured, 'that week-end was better than it would have been spent with Miss Atkinson and Mother watching television. Do let's hurry, Luke.'

To her surprise he said nonchalantly, 'We'll lunch first.'

'Lunch!'

'Don't be so impatient. I wasn't wasting my time on the telephone. Milton's due to leave for the hospital about two thirty. I want to arrive just as he's ready. Dressed and with his bag packed.'

'But Deirdre?'

'I know. It can't be helped.' Luke's face was intensely worried. 'But I think we can work on the assumption that if anything has happened to her it's happened by now. The next two hours won't be crucial.'

'You mean—in the night or early morning?'

Luke pressed her hand.

'You're being too imaginative. She's just been parked somewhere where her tongue can't run away with her. With her father, probably. That's what I believe. So let's have some coffee or a drink, anyway, if you don't want to eat. And you can tell me more about the day you thought you saw Mary pushing Milton. It was the day we were burgled, wasn't it?'

They talked of this and other things. Abby smoked several cigarettes and managed to eat a sandwich with her coffee. The waiting seemed interminable. But where her intuition had carried them a long way, now Luke's cool common sense prevailed.

They planned their approach to the Moffatts. When at last they stopped outside the old gray house, lizard-colored in the sun, they were both outwardly quite calm.

Someone had been watching, as usual, for the door opened before Luke had rung the bell.

Mary, dressed in a linen suit and looking even more pale and nervous than ever, appeared.

'Goodness, Luke, aren't you at work? Is something wrong?'

'Nothing at all except my bad manners. Abby has pointed out that I should have offered to drive Milton to the hospital, so I've come home specially.'

'And I'll collect Deirdre from school,' Abby added. 'I should have remembered that this morning, too.'

Mary backed away, half closing the door.

'There's no need, really. Milton always

prefers me to take him. Actually he insists. He hates a fuss. You know that. And Deirdre—'

'Abby, is that you? Abby, do you know what has happened? Oh dear, it's been such a shock.' Mrs. Moffatt was hurrying down the stairs with a ghostly tinkle of beads, and a flip flop of her bedroom slippers. 'Lola's taken Deirdre to boarding-school. Without saying a word to any of us. It seems she'd made arrangements some time ago, and thought she'd just do it like this to avoid a scene. You know how Lola and Milton both hate scenes. Not that Deirdre would have made one. She's not a coward, bless her. And now with Milton going off to hospital the house is going to be so quiet. It's terrible.'

'Shut up, Mother,' came Milton's voice curtly. 'You know who'd have made the scene about Deirdre's boarding-school. You.'

He had wheeled his chair into the hall. He was dressed in a dark gray suit with a discreet dark tie. From the waist up he looked like a successful business man, Abby thought, one of the kind who were driven to the city by their chauffeurs or caught jet airliners. A rug covered his legs.

'I've been saying for weeks that Deirdre must go to boarding-school,' he went on. 'She was completely out of hand. There's nothing to make a song and dance about now she's gone.'

His full, gray eyes rested on Abby. 'Deirdre

doesn't want sentiment. She doesn't understand it.'

'What have you done with her?' Abby asked, very softly.

She felt Luke's restraining hand on her arm. Mrs. Moffatt broke in eagerly.

'She is at a boarding-school, Abby. She really is. At least—'

'And I'm giving you a lift to the hospital, Milton,' said Luke. 'I won't take a refusal. I apologize for not offering sooner. Which hospital is it?'

'I told you I prefer my wife to take me.' Belatedly Milton added in a clipped voice, 'Thanks.'

Mary came forward.

'I always do, Luke. Milton really does prefer it. He hates other people seeing him helpless.'

'But not me,' said Luke. 'I'm not other people. I'm someone who's been in and out of your house for months. Sure, you come along, Mary, and give me directions. Do we take the chair?'

'But of course.' Mary's huge, frightened eyes sought her husband's. 'We can't manage without. He has to be lifted—' Her voice died away as she watched Luke cross the hall to stand behind Milton's chair, ready to push it.

Milton twisted round. There was a strange, violent look in his eyes.

'Take your hands off that chair! I've told you I won't be fussed over. Isn't it bad enough being helpless!'

'Sorry,' said Luke. He moved away, his hand accidentally catching the rug that covered Milton's legs. It fell off, disclosing a pair of immaculately trousered legs and polished leather shoes. Luke gave Milton a look of surprise.

'How far are you intending to walk?'

'Damn you, don't laugh at me!'

'He won't wear slippers,' Mary protested breathlessly. 'He says it's too much like being an invalid.'

Milton's face was tight with anger. 'You clumsy fool! Can't you leave me my vanities?'

'Sorry,' said Luke again. He looked at his watch.

'We'd better get moving, you know. I always allow a good hour to Sydney airport. The traffic's bad at this time of day. I believe the Comet's due to leave at three-thirty. Right?'

'The Comet!' gasped Mrs. Moffatt.

Luke ignored her.

'I have a feeling that hospital is in Singapore, you know. Let's take a look at your passport, Milton, and your air ticket. Are they in your breast pocket? After all, if you can't walk you're at my mercy, aren't you? Just as my wife was at yours and your hired killer's yesterday. Just as my brother was six months ago. Remember? The body in the harbor?'

Milton's face was gray. His eyes slid this way and that, the trapped lizard, Abby thought fleetingly. He looked beyond Abby, and that was when the strong, commanding voice came,

'Get out! Hurry! Get out!'

Taken by surprise, Abby turned to see Mary, her chin up, her deep, dark eyes smouldering. In the same moment Milton was out of the chair, sending it hurtling towards Luke as he leapt. Thrusting Abby and Mrs. Moffatt out of his way he made swiftly for the open door.

'Stop him!' Abby gasped, but her voice made no sound.

Surprisingly, Luke didn't move. He stood watching in an almost leisurely way. Watching not only Milton's flight but Mary's ashen, furious face, full of power.

Then another voice came from outside, old Jock's laconic drawl.

'I wouldn't try that, mate. You might get hurt.'

Old Jock who called everyone mate and threatened to shoot them in the back! For there he was, surprisingly erect and athletic, in a khaki shirt and trousers, holding a gun with careless efficiency.

Milton halted. A look of astonishment came over his face.

'You!' he exclaimed in disbelief. 'You scrounger!'

Jock grinned. 'That's me. Been keeping an eye on you with Mr. Fearon here.' He nodded towards Luke. 'You'd be as well to come quiet.

We've some more friends arriving.'

Abby watched dazedly as two uniformed police got out of a car and came towards Milton, the big, powerful man in the discreet gray suit so suitable for travelling.

It was then that Mary screamed and sank into a chair, covering her face.

'Oh, my goodness!' whispered Mrs. Moffatt. She tugged at her beads so frantically that they broke. In the silence following Mary's scream there was only the fragile tinkle of beads falling on the mosaic floor. A much more delicate sound than that of the footsteps Deirdre had heard in the night—the footsteps of an energetic, restless man confined all day to a chair and at the mercy of his greedy, dominating, megalomaniac wife.

'It was my fault,' said Abby, almost apologetically to Mrs. Moffatt. 'Deirdre told me about the cushions and rug made to look like someone in the chair. So that you could wheel an empty chair, Mary, and Milton could burgle Luke's and my house, trying to find a dangerous lipstick that had already been destroyed. Your psychology wasn't so good, after all. Did you think my husband would let me use another woman's lipstick?'

Mary lifted her wild face.

'Deirdre!' she exclaimed in tones of hate.

'Where is she?' Abby shook Mary's shoulder. 'Where is she?'

'Where she deserves to be, the little devil!'

Her eyes smouldered with fury. 'She's responsible for this. She's broken down all that I've spent so long building up. In another few months Milton and I would have had enough money to go away, live anywhere. But now—' she beat her fists on the chair '—when am I going to see my husband again?'

'Quite soon,' said Luke reassuringly. 'Sooner than you want to, probably, Rose Bay.'

Mrs. Moffatt gave a great gasp.

'But you're wrong, Luke! That woman's in Singapore. I know. She looks after us.'

Then she looked intensely guilty, and Luke had to say comfortingly, 'We know all about that, Mrs. Moffatt. But she isn't in Singapore, you know. It's only her husband who travels— when he isn't masquerading as a cripple. Come along, Mary. You're wanted.'

Fascinatedly Abby watched her stand erect. She saw her walk slowly and fatalistically towards the waiting police, her pale face a mask, only her eyes burning with all her perpetually untold feelings.

'Never trust the quiet ones,' said Luke. 'They blow up some time.' He looked very tired as he turned to Abby and Mrs. Moffatt. 'We'd better go home and have some tea. Come along, Mrs. Moffatt. Never mind your beads. They can be mended. Luckily some things can.'

It was Luke who made the tea, and together, in their pleasant sitting-room, he and

Abby persuaded Mrs. Moffatt to drink some. Luke had assured her that she would neither be arrested nor cut off at once from the drug she craved. She sat winding her thin, brown hands together and looking into space. Once she said, 'Whatever they say, I do love Deirdre.'

'Of course you do, Mrs. Moffatt. We'll soon have Deirdre back. The police are on to that.'

'What I don't understand,' said Abby, 'is why they went to such elaborate care to get me out of the house the day they wanted to burgle us. I was out all morning, as they knew. Why wasn't it done then?'

'Jock was watching,' said Luke simply. 'He didn't go to work until the afternoon. By that time you were back. So Mary had to ring you up. Anyway, she probably enjoyed that little bit of stageplay of letting you think she was wheeling Milton home in his chair. It was a good alibi for them all. Did you know Milton wasn't a cripple, Mrs. Moffatt?'

The frizzled gray head shook energetically.

'No! They fooled me about that. I didn't believe Deirdre when she said someone walked in the night. I never heard anything.'

When the telephone rang she sat stiffly upright, waiting to see who it was. So did Abby, until Luke came back to say that Lola had been picked up at her beauty salon.

'It created a furore among the clients, I believe,' he said tiredly, and Abby knew that, little as he cared for Lola with her brazen gaiety and her slim body, and the greediness for money that she shared with her sister, he hated this happening to a woman. He hated the whole thing with a weary despair.

'Both of them. Both of my girls,' said Mrs. Moffatt quietly. Presently she added, 'Mary always wanted to go on the stage. She was very good at acting. But there wasn't an opportunity and I suppose she was bitter and frustrated. She was very strong-willed beneath that quietness, you know. Very strong-willed. She must have pretended all that nervousness of Milton. It was part of her act, I suppose.' The old lady looked bewildered. 'Milton wasn't a cripple when he married her. They lived in Darwin, and she said that was where he had the car accident. He had been an importer and he had to give up his business. Mary asked if they could come here since he needed hospital treatment every now and then. She said money would be no trouble, and it wasn't. I thought Milton must have private means, but of course now I know better.'

She sighed deeply, looking guilty and ashamed again.

'Mary started me on the stuff about a year ago. She said it was good for depressions and headaches, it would make me feel young and gay. I loved being a young girl, you know, and I'd never had much of that either, with my husband dying so soon, leaving me with two babies. I'm only fifty-six now, although I know I look nearly eighty. It's this horrible stuff that now I can't do without.'

'And what about Lola?' Luke asked quietly.

'Poor Lola. She always wanted to get rich quick, and her marriage had been a failure. Not that Reg isn't still around, but he won't live here, and he's not one for responsibility or children. He's a chemist, you know. He's been very useful, Mary tells me. Making our fortunes, she says! Reg! I always thought he was such a weak creature. But it's so easy to be corrupted. So easy.'

The telephone rang again. When Luke came back Abby looked up eagerly. It must be about Deirdre this time.

But Luke shook his head. Abby saw the tautness of his face.

'What, Luke?'

'Milton. When they stopped to pay the toll on the bridge he made a break for it.'

Abby waited, remembering those great girders, the ominous shadow over the water, the inescapable feeling of doom the bridge had given her. She had had some strange kind of precognition, she realized. Now she knew what Luke was going to say.

'He succeeded in getting out of the car, but was knocked down by one coming the other way.' Presently he went on, 'Perhaps being a cripple in a wheel-chair was safer, after all. By the way, they've picked up Lola's husband, your fish-faced friend. But Deirdre wasn't in his rooms.'

'Then where is she? Didn't Lola say?'

Two of the kookaburras had come to perch in the jacaranda tree. The third was tapping at the window. But surely it hadn't become that confident and clever!

Abby turned sharply.

'Deirdre!' she cried.

Deirdre's face, thin and foxy, was pressed against the pane. When Abby opened the window she said in her blasé way,

'You took long enough to hear me. What are you all talking about so hard?'

Her face was grubby and faintly tear-stained, her hair hanging in strings. But she said perkily,

'I told him I'd escape and I did. The old bastard!'

'Deirdre!' exclaimed her grandmother, shocked.

'So he is. If that's my father, I'm sorry I met him.'

Luke lifted her up and set her in an easy chair.

'A cold drink, do you think, Abby. Lemonade?'

'Lime,' said Deirdre dispassionately. She waited for the drink and swallowed it thirstily. Mrs. Moffatt mopped at her tears.

'It's just us left, Deirdre. Did you know?'

Deirdre looked astonished.

'What's happened to old Milton? Did he tell you I saw him walking last night? Fancy sitting in that old chair when he could walk! He was wild with me for seeing him. That's why Mummy took me to my father today. But it wasn't much good. We didn't like each other. He kept telling me to shut up. So when he went out to get cigarettes I ran away.'

'But how did you find your way home?' Abby asked.

'I thumbed a lift. It's easy. Lots of kids do it.'

Abby began to laugh unsteadily.

'Luke, we don't have to worry about Deirdre. In fact, I think boarding-school is the answer.'

Deirdre looked from one to the other.

'What about Gran?'

'Gran will be going away for a while,' Luke said. 'She isn't well and needs treatment.'

'What about—Mummy?'

'She'll be away for a while, too.'

'Everybody! Good heavens!' Deirdre shrugged fatalistically. She swallowed the last drops of her drink. 'Actually, I've always wanted to go to boarding-school. I just hope—' She stopped and her eyes slid away.

'Hope what?' Luke insisted.

'That Abby might come and see me sometimes,' Deirdre mumbled self-consciously.

'Of course I will!' said Abby warmly.

258

Luke rubbed his hand in Deirdre's hair.

'Perceptive little brat, aren't you? You know who the nicest people are.'

Deirdre looked up, grinning with all her old bounce. In the brief silence a thread of music drifted up from the river.

But I love only you-oo, I love only you . . .

'Jock's home!' Abby exclaimed, and hurried out on to the patio to wave to the scrawny, half-naked figure in his shabby boat.

A lizard flashed in a long, gray streak across the sun-warm stones. The river was green and sluggish, the scent of the gums fragrant, like lavender.

A bird flew across Abby's vision, one of the kookaburras inviting her notice. When she ignored it, it settled in the jacaranda with its two companions and they all lifted their creamy throats and began to laugh.

The familiar sound was no longer shocking. It had become part of her life here, and consequently was quaintly original and amusing and completely acceptable . . .